# Minor Magic

*Book Seven of the Xoe Meyers Series*

## Sara C. Roethle

## *Dedication*

*To all of the readers who have stuck with this series over the years. I can't express my gratitude to all of you for helping to make my dream career a reality. So thank you, thank you, thank you!*

# Chapter 1

With one hand on the steering wheel, I held the other toward Chase in the passenger's seat, waiting for him to hand me the coffee he was totally hogging. "Tell me again why we decided to just share a cup?" I questioned.

I caught a glimpse of his smile, his tired dark gray eyes, and his slightly curly black hair, then turned my gaze back to the desolate highway ahead of us. Not that I have anything against Nevada, but it's not the nicest state to drive through, especially midday.

"When we buy two cups you drink all of yours, then move on to mine," he explained for the hundredth time. "This way we keep you from getting over-caffeinated."

"And *no one* wants Xoe over-caffeinated," Lucy added from the seat behind Chase.

"We have bigger problems," Allison groaned from the seat directly behind me. "Xoe, I think your dog has gas."

We all groaned as the vehicle filled up with a pungent stench. My Dalmatian, Alexius, gave a happy yip from his seat between Lucy and Allison.

"Well you two shouldn't have fed him all of

those potato chips," I chided, pushing my way too long blonde hair behind my ear. After an eventful winter spent mostly in the demon underground, my hair had darkened from white-blonde to ash. I was in need of a cut and some sun.

"He came from the spirit world with you when you returned from the dead," Allison countered, "I thought he could handle a few chips."

We all groaned as the car once again filled up with Alexius' stench.

"I think it's time to stop for lunch," I sighed, holding one hand up to cover my nose while I steered with the other.

"Yes please!" everyone else said in unison.

Alexius yipped again excitedly. For a spirit guide, he sure acted like a normal dog. He'd come into my possession when I'd *died* in the dream world. I'd been able to briefly see my father during that time. Alexius had been there to lead my spirit to whatever afterlife might await, but my dad had prevented me from going. We'd basically broken all the rules, and my best guess was that Alexius had nowhere to go after I refused to follow him. Thus, he'd somehow hitched a ride with me back to the real world and physically appeared.

A rest stop with a diner came into view, and I turned on my blinker then exited the highway. As we pulled into the parking lot I saw that the diner, which looked like something out of *Happy Days*, had outdoor seating where we could bring Alexius. Perfect. The weather was nice outside, but I still felt bad making him wait in the car, even if the temperature would be comfortable with the windows rolled down. I'd never been a pet owner before, but I'd turned into one of those annoying people who treat their pets like children. I wouldn't leave a child in the car, therefore I wouldn't leave the dog.

I pulled Allison's new red crossover vehicle into one of many free parking spaces. I had a feeling Allison had only volunteered the vehicle to ensure her presence on our road trip, but it was big enough to fit our luggage and passengers comfortably, and small enough to not kill us on gas mileage, so I'd happily agreed. Plus, it was fun watching her cringe any time we hit a pothole, and she practically screamed any time a branch threatened her shiny red paint job.

I parked and we all piled out of the vehicle. Lucy kept hold of Alexius' neon-green leash, attached to his matching neon collar as we walked across the asphalt to approach the diner. Why neon green? I'd read it was the best way to keep little Alexius from getting hit by a car. It just wouldn't be right to have him go out in such a mundane way after traveling all the way from the spirit world.

Chase took my hand as we walked, sending a little thrill up my bare arm, and not just from the touch. Ever since Chase found out that he could see ghosts, there always seemed to be an extra little zing of otherworldly energy hanging around him, like the ghosts were reaching out for attention. He was doing his best to ignore his newfound gifts, despite his brother Sam's assurances that they'd only get stronger.

I squinted my eyes against the springtime sun, taking a seat at one of the round tables in front of the diner. The tables had large umbrellas to shield them, but I'd ended up in the wrong seat.

Seeing my irritated frown as I blinked up at the sun, Lucy said, "Let's switch tables before Xoe burns the establishment to the ground."

I stood. "I can control my powers very well now, thank you." It was true. I'd been practicing.

We moved to another, more shaded table. I sat, smoothing my khaki shorts under my legs, then Lucy handed me Alexius' leash. Everyone else left me to go inside to order. I trusted Chase to not buy me anything healthy.

With a sigh, I pulled a manilla folder out of my large canvas purse. I'd gone over its contents a million times, but one more couldn't hurt. It was the entire reason for our trip, after all.

I placed the folder on the plastic tablecloth and opened it, scanning over my dad's research, which was confusing, at best. All I knew was that we were looking for a demon named Art, and I was pretty sure he was my relative. Maybe Art would know why my dad thought I was in danger. Danger that might have had nothing to do with the psychotic ghost of my grandmother.

Lucy and Allison only had one week off school for Spring Break, so we were making a mad dash all the way down to Nevada, taking turns driving throughout the day.

I heard footsteps behind me, then turned to see Allison and Lucy approaching. Of course they'd made Chase wait inside for the food. Lucy placed what looked like iced tea in front of me, then sat with her own drink. She flipped her long, black braid over her shoulder, eyeing the folder on the table.

Allison reached in front of me from the other side and shut the folder as she sat, sipping her drink through a plastic straw. "No more brooding over the info, Xoe. We'll find Art and we'll get some real answers."

"*If* we can find Art," I sighed.

If he'd lived in the underground, like most demons, we could have easily found Art with Sam's help, but he'd left over one hundred years ago, according to what little information Sam had been able to find. Why he left was anyone's guess. He had to have at least a small amount of human blood to leave at all, but that didn't tell me much. There were plenty of half-demons in the world.

Lucy reached over and patted Alexius, who panted happily beside my chair. "Maybe Alexius can sniff him out," she said, grinning down at the dog. She'd bonded much more with Alexius than Allison had.

Allison snorted, then pushed her chin-length, honey blonde hair out of her face. "Yeah, maybe the dog will be good for something after all."

Case in point. Allison had more snide comments for Alexius than she had for *me*, which was really saying something.

"He's good for plenty of things," I argued, taking my turn at patting Alexius' head.

"Like what?" Allison asked. Not waiting for my answer, she pulled her cell phone out of her purse to rapidly type a text.

I looked down at Alexius' happy face and felt an odd mixture of love and sadness. He'd been there the last time I saw my dad, in the spirit world, and had been my comfort in coming to terms with never seeing him again. In many ways, the dog felt like the last piece of my father I had left.

"He's good at being my buddy," I joked, "and that's good enough for me."

Allison sighed and continued texting. Probably talking to Max, who had not been pleased that he couldn't come on our trip. I needed him on another task. It was too soon to entirely abandon my new werewolf pack members, Emma and Siobhan, not that Siobhan really cared. Devin had stayed in Shelby to babysit, and had demanded that at least two other pack members remain behind. Since I wanted Lucy to come more than anyone, Lela and Max were chosen as co-babysitters.

I turned my attention away from Alexius to find Lucy leafing through a text book.

"Hey no homework!" Allison chided, staring at Lucy. "It's Spring Break."

Lucy glanced up from her textbook and rolled her eyes. "*Some* of us want to get into a good college."

Allison frowned and did her signature hair-flip,

which was less effective with her now-short hair. "Or you could just stay in Shelby and go to community college with me."

"PSU is only an hour away," Lucy argued. "We could both go and carpool together."

I leaned back in my seat. "Ah for the days where problems were as simple as deciding what college to attend," I mused out loud.

"Oh come on," Allison said, turning her honey-brown gaze to me. "I'd much rather be worrying about the vampire blood in my system and a demon-ey mystery than college."

Lucy scowled. "Way to be blunt, Allison."

"It's fine," I sighed.

Allison was only telling the truth. In all likelihood the vampire blood Jason and Chase had slipped me before I died in the dream world would have no effect. I'd been brought back to life, after all. Chase and my dad had done the same job the vampire blood would have done, except without the added effect of becoming a vampire. Could a demon even become a vampire? I hoped to never find out the answer to that question.

"It's not too late to consider college yourself," Lucy added, turning her gaze to me. "Once you take your GED you can start applying."

I shook my head. "No thanks. It's a demon's life for me."

"See?" Allison said. "Your life is totally better than mine."

"If you say so," I laughed.

Allison was still hell-bent on becoming something other than human. I understood her feeling left out since her two best friends were a werewolf and a demon, and her boyfriend a werewolf too, but I still didn't agree with her. Luckily no one in my pack was willing to make her a wolf, nor was Jason willing to make her a vampire.

The smell of fried food preceded Chase's arrival. He placed a tray on the table filled with baskets of french fries, two burgers, chicken strips, and a grilled cheese with a ridiculous amount of pickles on the side. He removed the grilled cheese plate and placed it in front of me.

"You really do know the way to my heart," I commented, looking down at the exact meal I would have wanted had I thought to ask for it.

He smiled as he took his burger plate. "Or at least the way to your stomach."

Lucy took the other burger plate, and Allison the chicken.

Alexius whined, and we all turned as one to look at Allison.

She glared at us.

"You know Alexius *loves* chicken strips," I pressed.

She bowed her head in defeat, then handed me one of her chicken strips to feed to the dog. "And you guys wonder why I don't like him," she muttered.

Alexius didn't seem to catch her rude comment, and gladly accepted the chicken strip.

The rest of us dug into our food. Just four

normal friends and a dog on a road trip. Anyone looking at us wouldn't think twice.

If only they knew the truth.

## Chapter 2

The next morning we reached our destination. At least, I hoped it was our destination. We only had a single address to go on from my dad's files, marked *Art?.*

"Wow," Allison muttered as we drove through the bland streets of Spring Valley, Nevada, "this is bleak."

"Tell me about it," I muttered, wishing Art had chosen a nicer place to take up residence. Not that it was a rundown area or anything, but the closely placed residences, lacking in surrounding vegetation save random prickly shrubs or cacti, were nothing like what we were used to seeing in Shelby, Oregon.

My phone's GPS directed us past nicer houses with identically landscaped front yards, then past some storage buildings, all the way to a small RV park. The park was mostly full, undoubtedly due to spring weather, the ungodly heat I'd heard so much about yet to set in. Hopefully it would stay temperate for our entire trip. None of us Pacific Northwesterners faired well in the heat.

"This is it," Chase said, holding my phone up in front of his face.

He'd put on his normal jeans and flannel that

morning, which I had a feeling he'd soon regret. Just because we wouldn't be around for the hundred plus temperatures, didn't mean it wouldn't still be hot. The rest of us were in shorts and lightweight teeshirts, baring our pasty legs to the Southwestern sun. Of course, Lucy wasn't really pasty. She looked just fine in shorts even though her olive legs rarely saw the sun.

I pulled the car into the last space left in the small parking area in front of the lobby, then glanced at Chase. "That paper doesn't say anything about which trailer we're looking for, does it?"

Chase lifted the paper from my dad's file from his lap and looked it over. "Nope, just the address. Maybe we can ask in the lobby if anyone named Art is registered."

I shrugged. "Worth a shot."

I shut off the engine and we all exited the car. Lucy and Allison stayed outside with Alexius while Chase and I approached the front office, which was actually just a small mobile home with the words *Office* tacked above the front door. Floral curtains shielded the windows amidst the white siding of the structure, and a barbecue rested out front beside two lounge chairs. Cozy. Kind of. It would have been nicer if the whole lot wasn't composed of red dirt that would stain anything it touched, including the bottom edges of the mobile homes and RVs. I was glad my sneakers were already well worn and stained with dirt, else I might have feared their demise.

Chase stood silently beside me as I smoothed

my hands over my blonde ponytail, hoping I looked moderately presentable, then knocked on the door.

A moment later, it swung inward, revealing a man in his mid-sixties, wearing a short-sleeved pastel plaid shirt, khaki shorts, leather loafers with tassels, and a wide, friendly smile.

Lucy suddenly appeared by my other side, as if by magic. Or werewolf speed.

I turned my head to her. She stared at the man. Following her gaze, I saw the man's smile slowly melt from his face. Alexius barked behind us. Looking over my shoulder, I saw Allison gripping his leash back by the car as he struggled against her.

"He's a werewolf," Lucy muttered, drawing my attention back to her.

"And so are you," the man replied quietly, his blue eyes trained on Lucy.

"So, ah," I began, "Can you tell me if anyone named Art is currently staying here?"

He continued to stare at Lucy, ignoring me. "You shouldn't be traveling without your pack," he growled at her. "Someone might think you're a rogue and . . . eliminate you."

"I'm with my pack leader," she growled back, nodding toward me.

The man turned his glare to me, making me wonder if his previous friendliness had only been my imagination. "You're not a wolf."

"How very observant of you," I replied. "We're looking for a man named Art."

"I'm not looking to become a part of any demon

business," he replied.

My eyes widened. Had he recognized my scent? Any wolf who'd been in previous contact with a demon would recognize it, but demons were a little more rare than werewolves. Most werewolves would go their entire lives without meeting someone with enough demon blood to smell different. Maybe he'd gotten to know the smell from Art.

"Well if you tell me where Art is," I countered, "we will gladly leave you alone."

He flicked his gaze back to Lucy. "I'm going to have to report your *illegal* presence."

Lucy sighed. "I *told* you, I'm with my pack leader. Leaders don't have to declare their presence in a new state, and they can bring an entourage of up to three wolves."

He seemed confused.

I rolled my eyes. I didn't exactly want to alert Art or anyone else of my presence, but I also needed t o *find* Art, and I had a feeling our new friend wouldn't take kindly to Lucy sniffing around the trailers for demon scent. "My name is Xoe Meyers," I explained. "I'm the leader of the Shelby, Oregon pack, and I'm completely within my rights to be here. In fact, I believe I'm completely within my rights to demand answers from you, unless you yourself are a pack leader."

His eyes widened, and suddenly fear replaced hostility in his expression. "I'll tell you whatever you need to know, just please don't report me to Abel. I know you and him are close."

I sighed, but didn't correct him. I wouldn't call my relationship with Abel *close*, but it didn't hurt to have all the wolves in the Western United States thinking I was in good with the Alpha of the entire district. Okay, so I *was* in good with him, but not by choice. He'd even given me an ugly braided bracelet that signified his protection. Should any wolf attack me, they'd be answering to Abel. The man before us eyed that bracelet now.

"Just tell me where Art is and I won't report you," I replied, though really I had no intention of reporting him unless he actually attacked me. Werewolf politics were a pain. The less I was involved in them, the better. Plus I didn't want everyone thinking I was a tattle tail.

He pointed to a trailer near the back of the lot. "I haven't seen Art in a few weeks, but that's his trailer. I see a woman coming and going sometimes, but I don't know her name."

I nodded. "Thanks, and please don't tell anyone we're here."

"Yes ma'm," he replied instantly.

I turned to hide my blush. I did *not* need men in their sixties calling me *ma'm*. It was just too weird.

He quickly shut the door and left us to our business.

I turned my gaze to Lucy. "Thanks for the weirdness, little miss alpha."

She looked down at her feet, embarrassed. "Sorry, my instincts jump in at the strangest times."

I patted her shoulder and let it go. I knew it

wasn't easy being a werewolf, let alone a werewolf with teenage girl hormones making your instincts go haywire. Teen girls were moody enough as it was. I should know since I'm one of them.

Allison moved to join us as I led the way to Art's RV, but I motioned for her to stay back with Alexius, ignoring her sudden glare. Since she was human, she couldn't take nearly as much damage as the rest of us, much to her chagrin. I didn't need her stepping out front to get attacked before any of us could save her.

The RV we approached had definitely seen better days. The siding was falling off in places, and the lowest metal step leading up to the water-stained door was missing. The hot sun reflected off bare metal in places, blinding me if I looked at it wrong.

Chase knocked on the door, then stepped back to stand beside me. Lucy waited a few feet behind us.

No answer.

He knocked again.

Still no answer.

"The man did say he hadn't seen Art in weeks," he sighed. "Maybe this is a dead end."

I walked away from the door toward one of the trailer's small windows. It was too high up for me to see much without jumping, but the interior was blocked out with heavy blue curtains regardless. I circled the rest of the trailer, just in case, then met Chase and Lucy back by the front door.

I stepped forward and tried the knob.

"*Xoe*," Lucy whispered harshly. "You can't just

open the door. It's private property."

"Actually," I whispered, "I can't just open the door because it's locked. Stand guard, will you?"

Her eyes widened. "Xoe, breaking and entering is illegal," she rasped.

"Yes it is," I replied.

I stole a quick glance around the RV park to make sure no one was watching, then reached for the knob again. Having no other choice, Chase and Lucy positioned themselves to block me from view as much as possible. I focused my powers on the knob, slowly heating the metal with a small amount of fire. I kept heating until the cheap metal melted.

I smiled and stepped back. *"Et Voila."*

Lucy turned her attention back to me while Chase continued to guard my back. I reached forward and pulled the door open, not being mindful of the hot metal since it couldn't burn me. The door swung outward, revealing the RV's dark interior.

I mounted the second step, the only one attached to the RV, and poked my head inside, mindful that someone might be waiting to attack me. I had just broken into a demon's RV, after all.

The interior was dark and still.

I stepped the rest of the way inside. The space appeared normal, if a little messy. There was a small kitchenette with a booth table for dining, and further back was the bed. To my left was a tiny bathroom. I was about to dismiss the place as empty, when I cast a final glance at the small stove, and the frying pan that rested there. It had scrambled eggs in it, and they looked fresh. I approached the pan and placed my hand near it. Still warm.

"Hello?" I called out softly as Chase stepped into the trailer behind me, leaving Lucy outside.

"It seems empty," Chase commented.

"There's someone here," I whispered.

There was a rustle from the direction of the bed, then a woman emerged from a pile of blankets and threw a knife right at my head.

I screeched as Chase pushed me aside, banging my hip into the small dining table.

The knife clattered harmlessly to the floor, and the woman stared at us in horror. She was probably around thirty, with mousy brown hair hanging limply around her face. She was thin, and seemed very frail, thought she'd thrown the knife with a good deal of force. She straightened her hot pink tank-top and gray sweatpants, but did not attack again. She appeared to be trembling.

"Any reason you just threw a knife at my head?" I questioned.

"I-I thought you were here to kill me," she stammered. "Are you?"

Well I *had* just broken into her RV, so I couldn't blame her for jumping to conclusions. I had called out though, so I didn't feel my intrusion merited a knife in the head.

"I'm just looking for Art," I explained. "Your door was . . . open, so I figured I'd check inside."

"P-please don't hurt me," she stammered.

I sighed. "Why would I hurt you? I already told

you why I'm here."

She suddenly slumped down onto the bed in defeat. "Art said that if you found me, you'd kill me."

I glanced at Chase, who shrugged.

"I don't even know who you are," I explained, "and I try not to go around killing strangers."

She cringed. "We're not exactly strangers."

I raised my eyebrows in surprise. "Come again?"

"If you don't know, then I'm not telling you," she stated boldly.

I stepped forward. "What happened to the please don't kill me bit?"

She instantly shrunk back. There was no reason she should be this afraid of me. I mean, I know I can be a bit cranky, but I only took part in the death of two demons. Scratch that, it was three, but few knew about the role I played in the death of Chase's ex girlfriend, Josie.

Her eyes shifted around the small space as if she might make a run for it, though we were blocking the only door. All she really had to do was call out for help and we'd be running ourselves to avoid police intervention, but she didn't.

"If I tell you where Art is," she began slowly, "do you promise to let me go unharmed?"

"Sure," I replied. Now we were getting somewhere.

"He's camped out in Red Rocks," she explained. "First exit after you enter the National Park's land. He's been hiding out ever since he heard your dad was trying to find him. Look for a red pick up truck, and you should be able to find him from there."

"You knew my dad?" I asked instantly.

"Knew?" she questioned. "Did something happen?"

I eyed her scrutinizingly. Either she was telling the truth about not knowing, or she was a very good actress. Of course, if she lived in the human world full time, it made sense that she might not have heard about my father's death.

"Never mind," I sighed. "Art better be where you say he is."

She nodded encouragingly.

I looked to Chase. "Shall we?"

He nodded, but seemed to be conflicted. He turned toward the woman. "You thought Xoe would know who you were. Why?"

The woman tensed, flicking her gaze between us. She licked her lips nervously, then admitted, "We're related," she said, her voice quavering. "Distantly. And that's all I have to say about it. Art can tell you the rest."

I narrowed my eyes at her. "If Art thinks I'm here to kill everyone, I doubt he's going to be in the mood to chat."

"B-but you said you weren't here to kill us," she stammered.

I sighed. "I'm not."

A knock sounded outside the trailer. "You okay, Suzie?" a man called.

"She's fine," I heard Lucy argue.

The woman, Suzie, glanced at the open door behind us, then back to me. She didn't answer the man who'd called out to her.

"I guess we'll be leaving," I stated, not wanting to get caught up in a conflict any more than we already had. I gave her my best cold stare. "But you better not be lying. I have a friend that can send ghosts to find you if you try to hide."

Suzie looked like she might faint.

I turned on my heel and headed for the door with Chase following close behind.

Outside waited a burly man with a buzz cut. His muscles strained underneath a white undershirt that had seen better days. Another resident?

Lucy stood behind his turned back. She caught my eye and mouthed, "*Werewolf*," while pointing at him.

"What is this, the supernatural trailer park?" I muttered as I walked past his glare.

"Yes," he answered simply, his gaze following me.

He watched us go, but didn't try to stop us. Feeling like we were now being watched from the inhabitants of all the nearby RVs and travel trailers, I hustled back to our vehicle where Allison waited with a bitter expression on her face.

Alexius yipped when he saw us.

I gave him a quick pat as I reached the driver's side door, then we all piled in.

The werewolf office man watched from his

window as I started the car and backed out of the spot. His expression was unreadable, but I had a feeling he was glad to see us go.

Normally I might be offended when people were glad to be rid of me, but it was beginning to become a theme in my life.

## Chapter 3

My cellphone buzzed again, rattling the center console like something alive. I glared at it, then turned my eyes back to the road.

"It might be important," Chase said evenly.

"Whatever it is, I'm sure Devin can handle it."

"You told him only to call you in case of emergencies," Lucy chimed in, nudging past Alexius to stick her head between the front seats.

I glanced down at the phone again as it buzzed with a new voicemail. "Fine," I grumbled. "One of you listen to it. I'm driving."

I did *not* want to deal with whatever Devin had to tell me. He'd been calling since we left the RV park. I really should have answered him right away, since he was watching over my werewolf pack, but didn't I have enough to deal with? Devin was a powerful werewolf, one of the most powerful around. What could I handle that he couldn't?

Lucy retrieved my phone. A moment later I could hear her gentle tapping as she typed in my voicemail password. Since I hated answering my phone, my friends all knew my voicemail password by heart. Kind of defeated the purpose of having a password at all, but whatever.

Another minute passed, and she ended the call and returned my phone to the console. "Emma's father is in town," she explained, "but she's the only one who has seen him. No one else can seem to find him."

I sighed. Just what we needed. Emma, one of my new pack members, came with a little bit of baggage. Her father, a human, was an abusive man. She lived with her foster parent Siobhan, another wolf who could protect Emma. Thing was, the *human* father had managed to elude all of the wolves after him. I had a feeling there was more to the dirtbag than what met the eye.

"Is she sure she saw him?" I asked, scanning our red rock surroundings for the turnoff. "Why didn't Jason call?"

Jason, my vampire ex boyfriend, had been hired to watch over Emma. I'd told him to call me if he needed.

"First," Lucy began, "I only listened to a message, so I couldn't really ask Devin if he was sure Emma saw her father. Second, Jason probably doesn't *want* to call you."

That last bit stung. I'd done my best to leave on good terms with Jason, but I was beginning to learn that it was uncomfortable to be friends with your ex. I glanced at Chase to see his frown, which he quickly hid as soon as he realized I was looking at him. The situation wasn't *just* uncomfortable for me.

It was all compounded by the fact that I was still mad at both Chase and Jason for slipping me some of

Jason's blood in case I died confronting my grandmother in the dream world. Would I have done the equivalent for either of them? Probably, but it didn't stop me from being a little peeved.

I put on the blinker and pulled over with a sigh. Not looking at anyone, I picked up my cell phone. Service was sketchy out in the middle of nowhere, but there was enough to make a call, unfortunately.

I opened my recent calls and selected Devin's number, then waited while it rang. I didn't have to wait long.

"It's about time," Devin chided, not even bothering to say hello. "We have problems."

I sighed. "Can you really not deal with a single human?"

"Hey, there's something wrong with this human. None of us can seem to find him, but he's harassed Emma twice now. Jason was outside of her house on one occasion, and outside of a restaurant where she was spending time with some friends on the other."

I took a deep breath, attempting to quell my irritation. "So what do you expect *me* to do about it? We're in Nevada."

"Can't you just poof back here and put your detective skills to work?"

"Detective skills?" I questioned.

"You and your little team seem to always figure out the mysteries," he explained. "And now you even have a dog to be your *Scooby Doo*."

"I can only travel with one person at a time," I replied tiredly, "and I'm not going to leave anyone alone out here for very long. We already accidentally encountered a demon and two werewolves at the supernatural RV park. Now we're in the middle of nowhere looking for someone in my dad's files, who apparently thinks I have reason to kill him."

Devin let out a long whistle. "You always seem to find trouble, don't you?"

I snorted. "It's a gift." I had a sudden thought. "Why don't you call Sam?"

I could sense his distaste, even over the phone. "Sam?" he questioned. "You mean Chase's much despised brother? Why would I call *him*?"

"He's trying to make amends so I'll want to kill him less," I explained. "He's even checking on Dorrie while we're away. His ghosts might be useful."

"You left your poor sparkly demon friend in *his* care?" he asked, ignoring my suggestion.

I sighed. "She's not a demon, and I'm quite sure she could beat him to a pulp if she needed." Thinking of Dorrie, I *was* a little worried. I really should call her to make sure Sam was doing his job.

"I'll call him," Devin agreed, but not like he liked it. "Text me his number after we hang up. And Xoe?"

"Yeah?"

"Hurry up and get your butt back here. Being pack leader is a pain."

I laughed. "Preaching to the choir, buddy."

He snorted, then hung up.

I texted him Sam's number, tossed my phone in the console, then pulled back onto the narrow highway, speeding onward.

Chase's eye bore into me, but I kept my gaze on the road. "You really think calling my brother is the best course of action?" he questioned finally.

"Sam, for some reason, wants to get in my good graces," I replied. "I think he'll help. If wolves can't find Emma's father, maybe ghosts can."

"Yeah but he wants to get in *your* good graces, not Devin's," he countered.

I laughed. "I'm sure Devin will find a way to make Sam believe getting in his good graces is the same thing as getting into mine."

Chase chuckled. "Devin does manage to talk his way through quite a bit."

I grinned. "It comes with the territory of being a smart ass."

"*You* would know," Allison chimed in from the backseat.

I rolled my eyes at her in the rearview mirror. "Oh please, everyone in this car would know all about being a smart ass."

"The turnoff," Lucy interrupted, pointing her finger between the front seats toward a green and white sign on the roadside.

I slowed the car and turned right, feeling suddenly nervous.

"How are we going to find him?" Allison asked.

I drove slowly, searching for signs of life. "I figured Lucy could sniff him out. Suzie, the lady in his RV, claimed he drove a red pick up truck out here. Once we locate it, we'll track his scent from there."

Speak of the devil. I spotted a dusty red pick up truck in the distance, parked aways down another turnoff. I maneuvered our vehicle toward it and sped along the bumpy dirt road. Red dust sprayed out from the wheels high enough to see it from our windows. I could sense Allison cringing behind me each time the car hit a particularly deep divot.

I slowed as we neared the truck, then parked beside it. We all wordlessly scanned the surrounding desert through the windshield and side windows. When no one saw any signs of life, we all piled out of the vehicle.

I walked around to the passenger side of our car, watching Lucy pace around the pickup truck, sniffing the air as she went.

I noticed with a start that I'd finally gotten used to her going all *wolfy*. It had unnerved me for the longest time, seeing my friend like that. Of course, I now spent most of my days around demons and other werewolves. Abnormal had become the norm.

Lucy finished her sniffing and returned to us. "I've got the scent. Let's go."

I nodded, then turned to Allison and Chase. "You two stay here, just in case he comes back while we're closing in on him. I have a feeling if he manages to drive away, he's going to be pretty impossible to find again."

Chase frowned, glanced at Allison, then nodded. I knew he wouldn't like me going off on my own, but Allison needed protection more than Lucy or I did.

I gave him a quick kiss on the cheek for not

giving me a hard time, then followed Lucy out into the desert. "Scream if there's trouble!" I called out as we walked away.

Now that I'd been to the area where we'd parked, I could *travel* back to it, along with Lucy. It was a neat trick to have, with the caveat that I couldn't *travel* to places I'd never been before. I had to be able to clearly envision my destination, and not just how it looked. I needed the feel of the place. The scents. *Everything*.

Our tennis shoes crunched on the rock ground as we left Chase and Allison behind. Now that I was taking the time to look, I found our surroundings breathtaking. Massive rock faces created a huge valley around us. The rocks were a deep red, a few shades darker than the clay-filled earth. The limited vegetation was prickly and offered no shade, but somehow seemed to add to the odd beauty of the place. However, I could have gone without the hot sun beating down on us.

Lucy's eyes were barely open as she followed her nose. Her black shorts and burgundy teeshirt were the wrong colors to be wearing under the hot sun, but she didn't seem to notice. Nor did she notice the beads of sweat slowly forming on her forehead. Following a scent took absolute concentration, or so I'd been told. It would have probably been easier to follow the scent in wolf form, but Lucy didn't transform unless she absolutely had to.

"We're close," she muttered.

I let out a shaky breath, glad we didn't have to

travel too far. Allison and Chase were well out of sight, but we'd probably still hear them if they yelled loud enough.

I scanned our surroundings, looking for some sign of Art. At first I noticed nothing out of the ordinary, but with a second glance, I picked out a small, tan tent, nestled on a ledge of rock.

"There," I whispered, though we were far enough off that whoever was in the tent probably wouldn't hear us. "You think that's him?"

She turned her head in the direction of the tent, and took a deep whiff. "It might be, but something smells *bad*."

I inhaled deeply through my nose and caught a brief whiff of a ripe, pungent odor, like the smell of long dead roadkill. "I have a bad feeling about this," I whispered.

Lucy nodded. "It might not be coming from the tent, though. Could just be dead animal. We'll have to get closer to see."

I grimaced. "But I don't want to get closer."

"Let's go." Lucy set off.

She was apparently much braver than I. I followed at her side, but slightly behind. If the smell was coming from the tent, I already had a good idea of what might be inside, and I didn't want to see it. I'd had enough death in my life already.

It only took us another seven or eight minutes to reach the tent, and the smell had intensified the entire way. I really didn't want to look inside, but we had to. It might not be Art, and once we called the police, we'd lose our chance to investigate.

"You do it," I said.

Lucy shook her head. "I am not touching that tent. If you want that zipper unzipped, you're going to have to do it yourself."

My face felt flushed with heat and nausea. I was doing my best to breath shallowly through my nose, but the smell was . . . permeating.

Knowing I had no other choice, I knelt down and reached a shaky hand toward the zipper. Nothing within the tent moved, but I still felt like something might jump out at me at any moment. I gripped the small metal toggle, warm from the sun, and slowly unzipped the tent, then reeled back at what I saw.

I'd never met nor seen a picture of Art to identify him, but it wouldn't have mattered. The body in the tent was so disfigured, there would have been no identifying it anyway.

I scurried away from the tent, fighting the urge to vomit.

A few moments later, Lucy came to stand beside me as I rested on my hands and knees. She crouched down to my level, then held out a worn leather journal.

I turned wide eyes to her. "Where did that come from?"

"It was in the tent."

"You reached into that tent!" I exclaimed, horrified that she'd put her hand anywhere near the decaying corpse.

"I saw the journal when I looked inside," she

explained, "and I had a feeling we'd want to hide it before we called the police. If it doesn't belong to Art, then we'll turn it in anonymously."

I grabbed the offered journal then forced myself to my feet, taking a few more steps away from the tent. "How are you so calm?"

She shrugged. "I'm good under pressure. I'll freak out later. Really, I'm surprised you're so freaked out. You've seen dead bodies before."

"Not *rotted* ones," I muttered, glancing down at the journal in my hands. There were no signs of blood or anything else on it, but I still felt the overwhelming urge to drop it in the dirt and run away to take a shower.

"Should we look for any more clues?" Lucy asked, glancing back at the tent.

"Nope," I replied instantly.

"But there might be evidence as to who murdered him," she argued.

I began to walk farther away from tent. "What makes you think he was murdered?" I asked, suddenly curious.

"He was covered in blood, Xoe."

I kept walking. "He could have gotten injured, then maybe a wild animal finished him off."

She smirked. "And zipped the tent back up after it was done with its supper?"

I would not vomit. I would not vomit. "Maybe he tried to hide in the tent from the animal, and bled out." I wasn't sure *why* I didn't want it to be murder. I guess because it made things more complicated. We might have to deal with a killer on top of everything else.

"There was a knife sticking out of his chest," she explained.

I flashed back on the corpse and suddenly felt a renewed need to vomit. I hadn't looked long enough to notice a knife.

"Okay," I conceded. "So he was murdered. We're still better off leaving any other evidence in the hands of the police. We don't have the forensic tools necessary to track a murderer."

Lucy stopped walking. "I think we should call Abel instead of the police. Really, if this is demon business, it should be taken care of by demons."

I stared at her, jaw agape. Little Lucy, who was so afraid of breaking the law, was suggesting we *not* report a murder.

Okay, so I'd failed to report murders in the past, but only when I was involved.

"Plus," she added. "If we can preserve the murder weapon, maybe Rose or Cynthia could do a spell to track its owner. It might be our only way of solving this mystery."

"You're creepy," I replied, starting to feel better now that we had some distance between us and the tent. She was also right. Rose and Cynthia were talented witches. They could probably help . . . not that they'd want to. They'd stayed as far away from me as possible after I'd forced them to summon a demon. Never mind that the demon was Sam.

"We'll go back to the car and call Abel," I

agreed. "Moab is only six or seven hours away from here. Maybe he'll come and take care of it all for us."

Lucy nodded. "He'll want to alert the local pack too, especially after what happened last time when supernaturals started disappearing."

I sighed. "If witches are kidnapping supernaturals again to try stealing their powers, I'm going to be pissed."

Lucy gently punched my shoulder playfully. "Now there's the Xoe I know and love."

I smiled and looked down at the journal in my hands, feeling better. As soon as we called Abel and distanced ourselves from the scene of the crime, I'd go through it. Hopefully there'd be some worthwhile information.

Let the mysterious case of the murdered demon and the leather bound journal commence.

## Chapter 4

"Why do these odd occurrences seem to follow you around?" Abel's voice sighed over the phone.

"It's not like I do it on purpose," I grumbled.

Allison was taking her turn at driving with Lucy as copilot. I'd felt shaky since we returned to the car, having lost the initial adrenaline boost after finding the dead body, and was glad to cozy up in the back seat with Chase and Alexius. Chase held my cold, clammy hand as I used the other to keep the phone plastered to my ear.

"Give me directions to find the corpse," Abel sighed.

I gave him clear directions, then asked, "Are you coming yourself?"

"Not yet," he replied. "I'll send a few wolves to take care of the body. My guess is this won't be a mystery the police are equipped to handle, and we don't want them making any connections between you and the dead man, if you are in fact kin."

"If we're related through my demon father, there's probably no record of it," I explained tiredly.

"Be that as it may, I don't want a repeat of what happened *last* time."

I sighed. "Lucy brought that up too. You really

think witches might be involved?"

"It's far too soon to tell. Probably not, but it's difficult to avoid a bit of paranoia."

"Nothing wrong with paranoia," I replied. "It keeps us alive."

He chuckled. "Amen to that. I recommend you find a hotel far from the murder scene. Take a look at that journal, and wait for me to contact you. If my people find any clues, you'll be the first to know."

I nodded, then realized he couldn't see it. "Okay," I confirmed, then hung up. Here I thought we were going to have a nice, information-getting road trip, and now we were about to be neck deep in a supernatural murder investigation.

I looked down at the journal in my lap, almost afraid to look inside. What if it held nothing important? What if it wasn't even Art's and I stole some poor, lost hiker's journal? There was only one way to find out.

I slipped my hand out of Chase's and opened it. I held it in front of my face, ignoring the gross feeling it gave me. I couldn't stop imagining it spending all that time in a tent with a dead guy. Only a few of the pages were filled with messy handwriting, but they instantly drew me in.

A few minutes went by as I read.

"Xoe?" Chase questioned, watching me.

I held up a finger and continued to read until I finished the few pages, then shut the journal and sat back against my seat, feeling slightly stunned. Alexius nudged the journal out of my lap so he could replace it with the front half of his body.

I turned wide eyes to Chase.

"What did you find out?" Lucy asked, turning around in her seat to look at me.

"Well my dad was right," I began numbly. "I was in danger. Still am, maybe."

Chase reached over and tugged the journal from my hand where it rested beside my leg. He started reading it while I continued to mull things over. Lucy eyed me impatiently, but I still needed a moment for it to sink in.

Once Chase had finished reading the few pages, he handed the journal to Lucy. She read them quickly, still turned around in her seat to dart occasional glances at me.

"Woah," she said as she finished.

"Would someone please tell me what's going on?" Allison snapped from the driver's seat.

Lucy's eyes remained on the journal, skimming it a second time as she explained, "Xoe and her father were apparently viewed as rather high up in the demon hierarchy. They got all of the good powers and respect, while their distant relatives ended up more human than demon. Too weak to survive in the demon underground, they fled to the human world where they had to live under the radar of human society."

I chewed on my fingernail in thought, then blurted, "It doesn't make sense though, why didn't my dad tell me all of this?" I turned to Chase. He'd known my dad longer than I had.

He shrugged. "You knew you had a strong

37

bloodline, but I think the existence of distant family members might have been news to your dad as well, which would explain why he'd be researching them. Maybe he'd only recently found out about them and was trying to uncover more information before he told everything to you, but he didn't get very far before . . . "

"My grandmother killed him," I finished for him. "I wonder if her reappearance was what caused my dad to start snooping. According to that journal, Art and a few others had been watching us for a while, and were obviously jealous. He made it seem like they tried to hurt us, but failed, and expected me or my dad to come after them."

"But neither of you even knew anything had happened," Chase observed. "You were too busy dealing with Bartimus, then your grandmother."

"So if this Art had a grudge against you," Lucy said thoughtfully, "maybe whoever killed him did you a favor."

Allison cleared her throat, keeping her eyes on the road ahead of us. "Then why didn't that demon in the RV park try to kill you?" she asked.

"Because they believed my dad and I had all of the power," I explained. "She wasn't strong enough to attack me on her own."

"She didn't really seem like she hated you," Chase countered. "In fact, she seemed like she felt kind of guilty."

"We need to go back and talk to her," I decided.

"If she's even still there," Lucy added.

I sighed. She was right. Suzie had probably high-tailed it out of there as soon as we left. "It's worth a shot. While we look for her, Abel's people will have a chance to investigate Art's tent to get some idea of who killed him. Given the circumstances, finding the murderer will probably be our best lead."

Lucy frowned, still looking back at me. "Hopefully we can manage it by the end of the week, before Allison and I have to get back to school."

Allison snorted. "C'mon, we can miss a few days. A murder investigation is much more exciting."

I watched as Lucy raised an eyebrow at her. "Don't want to get back to Max?"

Allison removed a hand from the wheel and waved her off. "The longer I'm gone, the more he'll miss me. I'm giving him something to look forward to."

I laughed, feeling slightly better. My friends tended to have that effect on me. I turned toward Chase. "Is that true? Should I run away for a while so you'll have a chance to miss me?"

"And let you get into trouble without me?" he questioned. "I think not. I've already missed out on plenty, hanging out with Sam to get this ghost-seeing situation under control."

I inhaled sharply as I had a sudden thought, then turned a mischievous grin to Chase.

He instantly shook his head. "Oh no, I know that smile. I'm not going to like whatever is coming next."

I smiled wider. "Well I was just thinking, you know, since Art recently died and all. If his ghost is still around, maybe we can summon it and ask it who killed him."

Chase sighed. "Most ghosts are just remaining energy. They don't have memories. Your grandmother was different. She stuck around on purpose, unable to let go of what happened to her."

"And my dad too," I added. "He managed to hang on for quite a while out of a need to protect me."

"Art could be hanging on for either of those reasons," Allison added. "Vengeance on who killed him, or a need to protect anyone else he cared about from big, bad Xoe."

Chase bit his lip, obviously not liking the idea.

My expression softened as I realized I was being an ass. Chase had discovered his abilities when I *died*, and they'd caused him nothing but discomfort ever since. For me to ask that he intentionally use them was beyond selfish.

I grabbed his hand and gave him an apologetic smile. "Even if he is around, he would probably only cause us more trouble," I announced. "For now, we should just question the living."

Lucy glanced at me, obviously suspicious of my sudden change of heart, then realization dawned on her face and she quickly turned around. Asking Chase to summon a ghost would have been like asking Lucy to go all wolfy just after she'd been attacked, and was still horrified with her new life.

"I'll try," Chase sighed, "but I should probably

call Sam first to ask just how to do it."

"It's okay," I argued. "Probably a bad idea."

He rolled his eyes at me. "I really should learn to control this new *gift* regardless. Plus, we need to call Sam anyways to make sure he's properly attending to Dorrie's needs."

I laughed. "She's probably already made him check out half the library for her."

He grinned. "And I imagine he has bloody fingers by now from all of the games of Checkers."

"I really must meet this Dorrie," Allison cut in. "Anyone capable of bossing Chase's brother around seems like my kind of girl."

I had been meaning to take Lucy and Allison underground to spend time with Dorrie, but we'd just been so busy. I was also worried Allison would be a bad influence on her. Dorrie was already a bit intense. Combining her energy with Allison's bad attitude was a recipe for disaster. Not that I said so out loud.

"Once we get back to Shelby, I'll bring you down for a visit," I assured.

"I'm holding you to that," Allison replied, taking the turn that would lead us back to the RV park.

Allison would take any opportunity she could get to explore the demon underground. She'd been down a few times before I acquired Dorrie, but demons really weren't supposed to bring humans into our city. I was yet to stand trial for any of my demonic crimes, but it could happen eventually. I wasn't even sure how the whole justice system worked, but it probably wouldn't go well for me without my dad around to help.

But that was a problem for another time. First, we had to deal with the fact that the RV park ahead of us was on fire.

"Well this is bad," Allison commented, parking the car a few yards away from the nearest fire truck.

There were several police cars present too, and it was evident everyone had just arrived. As we watched, the first of the fire hoses became active to begin spraying the out of control flames. Those evacuated from the park all waited out on the street, watching as their homes and possessions were destroyed. We all sat in the car and watched.

"Well I hope most of these people were just here on vacation and have homes elsewhere, or we just cost a lot of people all of their worldly possessions," Allison commented.

"We?" I questioned, leaning forward to peer out of the front windshield at the fire.

"You really think it's coincidence that the whole place goes up in flames right after we left?" she asked.

I sighed and slumped back against my seat as Alexius started to whine. At first I thought he was just upset by the fire and the smoky air beginning to surround us, then I realized someone was watching us. As quickly as I'd noticed her, she'd disappeared.

"Did you guys see that girl?" I questioned instantly, debating getting out of the car to follow her.

"No?" Chase and Lucy replied at the same time as Allison said, "What girl?"

I shook my head, then scanned the area where she'd been standing, across the road from the RV park, partially concealed by a dumpster. I'd only caught a quick glimpse of her, but I was pretty sure I recognized that face. It was difficult to forget a girl after she'd sliced you open and left you to bleed out in a public bathroom. Alexius had stopped whining as soon as she disappeared. Maybe he remembered her from the dream realm.

I looked past Alexius to meet Chase's eyes. "I think it was Nix."

He furrowed his brow in confusion, then glanced to where I'd been looking. He seemed deep in thought as he turned back to me. "But didn't we leave her in the dream realm? She disappeared shortly after you . . . you know . . . "

"Died," I finished for him. "I know, but I'm pretty sure it was her. Maybe someone summoned her out."

He stroked his chin in thought. "It's possible. Since she knew your grandmother, she knew about your ability to make portals to the dream realm. Maybe she had a back up plan in place, just on the off chance that she might get trapped there."

"Maybe," I muttered, still glancing around outside the car for her.

My gaze was drawn elsewhere as a police officer approached, herding away the evacuees and onlookers alike. He turned his gaze to Allison in the driver's seat and signaled for her to back the car away. They were probably widening the perimeter as they tried to get the fire under control.

Allison started the car and did as she was instructed, backing down the street far enough to turn around and head back the way we'd come. Even if Suzie was still around, we couldn't very well go about questioning the evacuees while the police looked on. They'd probably arrest us for suspected arson.

She turned left at the intersection, then continued driving as I mulled everything over.

"We should get a hotel, then call Abel," Lucy announced. "And Devin," she added. "If people are burning down trailer parks because of our presence we should warn the rest of the pack, just in case something happens to us."

I nodded my agreement as she looked back at me, but didn't speak. A million thoughts filtered through my mind, none of them good. Someone had murdered Art, and now had burned down an entire RV park just after we'd visited it. Had they been targeting his trailer to eliminate any evidence, and if so, why wait until after we'd already been there? His rotted corpse had been lying in that tent for at least a week. If they simply wanted to cover up any extra evidence, they would have done it right after they killed him. It had to be because of us. The only question was, what were they trying to hide? If Art had technically been my enemy, then was the enemy of my enemy my friend? I doubted it.

Like usual, we were up stink creek without a paddle nor a clue.

Allison took another turn, then pulled up to a

large chain hotel.

"Are we sure we want to stay this close to the scene of an arson?" Lucy questioned nervously.

"The better to lure out the perpetrators," Allison replied.

I could see the logic behind her decision, although whoever burned the park might just set the hotel ablaze while we were sleeping. Honestly, given the fact my skin couldn't get burned, I might survive a fire, but everyone else would not. Allison parked the car, leaving no room for arguments.

"Let's have someone keep watch at all times," I decided, "just in case."

Everyone nodded in agreement. Alexius tilted his head curiously. Hopefully the hotel was dog friendly.

As Chase slipped out of the car to purchase a room, I handed him my bank card. The card was still connected to Jason's account. When Abel paid me for taking care of a certain psychopathic werewolf, I'd had Jason deposit the money in an account connected to his, given I was only sixteen at the time and not eligible to have an account on my own. Now it was just awkward. How do you explain to your ex boyfriend whom you want to be friends with that you should probably change your banking situation? I shook my head and sighed. Not the time to think about it.

A few silent minutes later, Chase returned from the front office, key cards in hand. We spilled out of the car, gathered our luggage, then followed him up a nearby flight of stairs to our room. I tugged Alexius behind me while he attempted to stop and sniff every single step.

Chase unlocked the door as we reached it, holding it open for everyone to enter ahead of him. I entered, then dropped my bags on the bed nearest to the door, claiming it. My green duffle bag and faded gray backpack clashed with the ugly, geometric print bedspread, which clashed even more with the muted, multi-colored carpeting. Or maybe I was just looking at things with cranky eyes.

I turned around and smiled as Allison started ordering a pizza, her cellphone pressed to her ear. Surely pizza would brighten my mood.

Chase took my hand and gave it a tug, distracting me. "Let's go get some extra towels," he said. "They never leave enough for four people."

I nodded, then glanced at Allison and Lucy. They sat on the foot of the far bed, already flipping channels on the TV, with Alexius curled up contentedly at their feet.

I followed Chase outside, feeling uneasy. Logically I knew it was unlikely anyone would attack my friends in the few minutes we were gone, but the sick feeling in my stomach begged to differ.

Regardless, I went, but waited on the landing to hear the door shut and lock behind us before walking toward the stairs. I focused my attention on Chase's broad, green flannel clad back as he walked a few steps ahead of me. For some reason, I found myself wondering about his history again. Probably because I was still trying to figure out my own. He'd given me bits and pieces along the way. For instance, I knew that his mother was a Naga and his father a necro-demon, like Sam. The parents had gotten together for the purposes of procreation, and that was it. The mom had taken Chase, while the dad took Sam. Chase's mother had died when he was fifteen, at which point Sam found him, got him in a bunch of trouble, and their relationship had been tense ever since. Somewhere in there my dad had taken Chase under his wing, employing him to watch over his wayward daughter.

I hustled down the stairs to catch up to his side. "So my dad never said anything about Art, or any of our other family the whole time you knew him?"

He stopped walking and looked over at me, curiosity in his gray eyes. "Your dad kept a lot to himself. I just knew he had a daughter living in the human world, and he was worried you'd either get yourself into trouble, or some other demon would find out about your existence and try to use you."

I leaned my back against a support post near the stairs and gazed out at the sky. The smoke from the RV park fire could be seen not far off, making the air seem hazy. "It's just that I don't understand why I never even knew I had other demon family. I mean, it makes sense, plenty of people have distant cousins they've never met, but still, you'd think he would have mentioned it."

Chase shrugged, then leaned his back beside mine. "You know demon families don't act like human families. There's no true bond or loyalty there. Parents raise their offspring, hoping to create a powerful legacy, but there's no reason for cousins to get to know each other. Some siblings stick together, but that's about it."

"Like you and Sam?" I questioned.

He snorted. "I didn't even know Sam existed until we were teenagers, and we haven't exactly *stuck* together."

"He cares about you, though," I commented.

Chase turned his head and raised a dark eyebrow at me.

"Oh please," I continued, "Sam has not been trying to make amends just because he's afraid of me. He could disappear easily enough if he wanted to. He's staying around because of *you*."

"That's not how demons are," he muttered, looking down at his shoes.

"First," I began, holding a finger in the air, "I find your generalized opinions of demons mildly insulting, given that I'm one too. Second, *you* are living proof that your generalizations aren't entirely accurate."

He laughed and met my gaze. "Am I? How so?"

I rolled my eyes. "Correct me if I'm wrong, but I'm pretty sure you don't care about me just because of my bloodline. In fact, I'm quite sure you care about me in spite of it."

He waggled his eyebrows at me. "Or else I'm just trying to continue my own bloodline with someone powerful."

I shoved his shoulder playfully. "I think it's a bit soon to be talking about children. Maybe a few years down the road when people stop trying to kill me."

He wrapped an arm around me and pulled me close. "I'm pretty sure that time will never come. It's in your nature to piss people off."

I pulled away with a grin and grabbed his hand, then started tugging him toward the front office. "Weren't we supposed to be getting towels or something?"

He shrugged. "Nah, I just wanted a few minutes alone with you."

He tugged me back toward him, then wrapped me up in a hug. "I know it's tempting to somehow connect with your demon kin," he said softly against my hair, "but you need to remember that you and I are exceptions to demonkind, not the rule."

I pulled away just enough to look up and meet his eyes. "How'd you know what I was thinking?"

He lifted one shoulder in a half shrug. "I know family is important to you. If you find any long-lost members who aren't out to get you, you'll try to keep them."

"So?"

He sighed and kissed my forehead. "I just don't want you to be disappointed. Most demons aren't worth knowing."

I thought of his experiences with his family, and with his crazy ex, Josie. I could understand where he was coming from, but . . . "What if we find more exceptions to the rule?"

He laughed. "Then we'll give them a probationary period. If they go six months without trying to kill any of us, then maybe they're worth the risk."

I nodded, accepting his terms. I knew it was unlikely that any of my distant kin would desire a relationship with me, especially with the track record of extended family thus far, but a girl can hope, right?

# Chapter 5

We had just arrived back at the room with fresh towels when my cellphone buzzed in my pocket. I pulled it out and answered it while Chase held the door open for me to step inside.

Lucy and Allison were still sitting on the foot of their bed watching TV with Alexius at their feet. I waved at them to turn the volume down as Abel's voice filtered into my ear.

"You wouldn't happen to know anything about an RV park fire, would you?" he asked.

I cringed. "What, no, *Hey Xoe, how are you doing after finding that grisly corpse?*"

Abel sighed, then silently waited for me to answer.

"I didn't start it, if that's what you're asking," I grumped at him. "We were on our way back there when we saw the flames."

"So you *were* there?" he questioned. "I'd hoped Iva was mistaken."

"Iva?" I questioned, confused.

"The local pack leader," he explained. "She called an asked me to arrange a meeting with you."

I groaned. "Say it isn't so." I didn't want to go to any *meeting.*

He sighed again. "Trouble truly does seem to follow you, doesn't it?"

"That's what happens when *Trouble* is your middle name," I joked. I briefly considered telling him I'd spotted Nix, but I wasn't entirely sure it had been her. In all likelihood, she was still trapped in the dream realm.

"Did your people find the tent?" I asked, wanting to change the subject before he could blame me for the fire any further.

"Yes, but not much else, except enough lingering scent to verify that the corpse was a demon. They took care of the body and disposed of his truck, tent, and camping gear. He had few belongings with him, but we did, however, find a wallet."

"Wallet?" I questioned hopefully. At the very least, we could verify the dead man was indeed Art, and not some other demon writing about me in his journal.

"Arthur Merryweather," he replied. "We checked the address listed on the card, but it was old. Some nice human family living there now."

"Merryweather," I muttered to myself thoughtfully.

"I thought most demons don't even have last names?" he asked like it was a question.

"I have a last name," I replied snippishly.

He sighed again. I seemed to have that effect on him. "You know what I mean."

It was my turn to sigh. "Only those who remain underground forgo last names. Most half-demons have them. Though from what I've been able to find, Art was full-time underground before he fled, so the name is probably fake."

"It still might be linked to more information," he explained.

"And do we have the means to acquire that information?" I asked hopefully.

"We're looking into it, but for now you're going to have to meet with the local pack leader. She's a little pissed about the RV park. Several of her pack members lived there, along with a vampire and your demon friends."

I pinched my brow with my free hand as a headache began behind my eyes. I really didn't want to delve into any more werewolf politics.

Chase was eyeing me not-so-patiently, waiting for information.

"Please tell me I won't have to see the vampire too," I pleaded, resigned to my fate. It was more than enough to deal with a bunch of new wolves, I didn't want to add a vampire to the mix. Barring Jason, my experiences with vampires had not been the best. They tended to die around me.

"He's connected to the pack," Abel explained, "much like Jason is with yours. It would not surprise me if he's at the meeting."

"My day just gets better and better," I muttered.

Abel chuckled, then rattled off an address.

"Hold on," I snapped. "Let me get a pen."

I moved to the small square table between the two beds and searched the drawer, then pulled out a pad of paper and a pen. "Ready."

He repeated the address and I quickly jotted it down.

"What hotel are you at?" he questioned.

I paused for a moment, suddenly suspicious. "Why?"

"So I know where to get a room once I'm able to make it out there."

I pursed my lips in agitation, but acquiesced. He was coming to Nevada to help us, after all. The least I could do was let him stay in the same hotel as us.

He was silent for a moment, presumably writing down the hotel name.

"Your backup will meet you at the pack leader's home," he explained. "Be nice to them, because they're doing me a favor."

"Backup?"

He laughed. "You didn't think I'd send my favorite demon alpha into a den of wolves without a little protection, did you?"

"Just make sure I don't need to protect myself from the protection. I don't have a great track record for first impressions with new wolves."

He laughed again. "Just be your pleasant self, and I'm sure everything will be fine. Be there at 10 pm, and watch your back. There's still a murderer on the loose."

"Aye aye captain," I replied, but he had already hung up. Did all werewolves have horrible phone etiquette, or was I just lucky?

"What was that about vampires?" Allison asked

as I lowered the phone to my lap.

I flopped my back onto the bed and stared up at the ceiling. "That we have to go meet one along with a bunch of werewolves at 10 pm."

Chase sat beside me on the bed, gazing down at my pained expression. "Are we sure that's wise with just the four of us?"

"We'll have backup," I groaned, wanting nothing more than to pile into Allison's car and drive back home.

This was turning into a *total* disaster. The last time a scenario like this played when we were out of state, two vampires and a few werewolves had ended up dead, and I'd made an unsavory bargain with a flesh-eating demon. I'd also gotten the crap beaten out of me, and Chase had gotten mauled . . . several times.

"What about Art?" he pressed when I didn't explicate.

"No new info except a last name," I replied, clenching my eyes shut against my growing headache. "Abel is looking into it."

There was a knock on the door. Pizza, hopefully.

I kept my eyes closed as Chase rose to answer the door and pay. Moments later, the smell of pizza filled the room. My stomach groaned uncomfortably. Pizza wasn't going to be enough to brighten my mood after all.

I sat up, setting my phone beside me on the bed. Chase sat next to me, placing the pizza on the central nightstand. Lucy and Allison rested on the other bed across from us, like we were all sitting around a dining table, only there was just empty space between us, and the nightstand to my left and Lucy's right. Lucy opened the pizza box and began doling out slices on paper plates.

I took mine with a frown. My phone buzzed. I reluctantly rested my plate on my lap, hearing my stomach growl loudly. I reached for my phone by my thigh and handed it straight to Chase. "Answer it. I can't talk to anyone else right now."

He answered it quickly before the caller could hang up. After saying hello, he paused for several seconds, then handed the phone to me. "It's Jason."

Well that wasn't awkward at all.

I took the phone and held it to my ear. "Hey, what's up?"

"I just thought I'd check in," he explained, his voice sounding normal and not nearly as awkward as I felt. We hadn't spoken much since the vampire blood incident, but I couldn't really hold a grudge against him if I wasn't holding one against Chase.

"How's Emma?" I pressed on. "Devin called earlier and explained things."

"She's fine. A little scared, but Devin is surprisingly good at being a pack leader."

"Good," I replied with a laugh. "Maybe he'll want to continue the role even after we come back."

Jason was silent for a moment. "You know, that's not a terrible idea."

I paused. Was he serious? I hadn't even thought about it, but . . . "Maybe mention it next time you see him. Put the idea in his head."

I could sense his shock, even over the phone. "Seriously? You've defended your role as pack leader tooth and nail."

Ignoring the unintended werewolf pun, I sighed, "Only out of necessity, but this might work out a lot better for everyone."

He was silent again.

"Jason?" I questioned.

"It's nothing," he muttered, "just surprised how much you've changed."

"I can grow and evolve like everyone else," I stated haughtily.

He laughed. "Well then I look forward to seeing where you end up. Did Abel find anything out about the murder victim?"

Gee, Abel sure was chatty. The entire state of Oregon probably knew about Art's murder by now. "Not much," I replied, keeping my catty thoughts to myself, "but he's still looking. We're going to be meeting with the local werewolf pack while we wait."

"So I've heard. Be careful."

Word sure traveled fast, but that brought to mind another thought. "Abel said there's going to be a vampire there. Any advice?"

"Stay away from the pointy end," he joked.

I laughed. "Seriously though. Advice?"

"Don't set him or her on fire?"

I sighed. "You're incorrigible."

"I know. The only advice I have is to get in and out as quickly as possible, and watch your back.

And," he hesitated, "Please send me a quick text to let me know when you get out alive."

"Sure," I said with a smile. "Thanks for checking in."

"Of course," he replied, then hung up.

Didn't anyone say bye anymore?

"Emma is scared, but alright," I explained to everyone, then picked up my pizza to take a bite.

"Are you really thinking about giving up your role as pack leader?" Lucy questioned with a blank face, leaving me clueless to her opinion.

I thought for a moment, then nodded. I could admit, the thought had crossed my mind a time or two before, though I hadn't previously pegged Devin for the role. "Maybe. It's crossed my mind now and then, but I never really considered it because there was no one else I could trust to take on the danger of the job. I don't know why I didn't think of Devin, other than the fact that he's been against choosing a pack for years. He likes it in Shelby though, and he seems to enjoy being with the pack. He's strong enough to take care of things. I trust him to watch out for everyone."

Lucy nodded, seeming deep in thought.

I turned to Chase, who was eating his pizza silently. "What do you think?"

He placed his pizza back on his plate and smiled. "If I give you my opinion, do you promise not to refute it simply because it's what someone thinks is best for you?"

I held a hand to my chest as if wounded. "Do you truly think so little of me?"

He smirked. "No, but I *know* you. If people think something is a good choice for you, it's in your nature to figure out reasons to disagree."

Lucy and Allison both nodded in agreement.

I scowled at them. "Is this what mutiny feels like?"

They nodded again, adding wicked smiles.

I sighed and turned back to Chase. "I want your honest opinion, and I promise to not spite you."

"In that case, I think it's a great idea," he admitted. "You've been drowning in responsibilities this past year. You could use a break, and since it's Devin, I'm sure he'd be happy to still have you involved in the pack as much or as little as you wanted. Abel isn't going to like it, but I think if you're still associated with the wolves in some way, he'll deal with it."

I smirked. "Yeah, he just likes the threat of having a demon around. Although I can admit, it's also useful to have someone with access to information, who is also willing to dispose of bodies on my behalf."

Everyone laughed, and I just shook my head ruefully. I wasn't sure about my moral compass these days, but it had probably gone pretty far South when one of my main concerns was body disposal.

But hey, a girl's gotta have her priorities, right?

I took another bite of my pizza, feeling slightly better. I was still worried about the upcoming meeting, but maybe there was an end in sight with all of this werewolf stuff. Heck I was only seventeen. I should have been worrying about finals and applying for college, not werewolf politics.

I glanced at Chase and my friends as they chatted happily. I knew Lucy and Allison had their plans all sorted out, but what about me and Chase? He'd basically lost his *job* when my dad died. I knew he'd been helping Sam in the information dealing business to earn extra money, but was that really what he wanted to do? I'd basically been living off money from the bounty on Dan, the psycho who turned Lucy into a wolf, and I'd inherited some from my dad, but it wouldn't last forever. I needed to find *something*. I was beginning to feel that college wasn't in the cards, but what then? It was something I needed to figure out, and maybe if I was no longer a werewolf pack leader, I'd have time to do that.

I startled as I realized Chase was watching me while I'd become entrenched in my own thoughts.

He raised an eyebrow at me. "You know you mutter to yourself when you get too deep in your own head?"

I blushed. "I was just thinking about what I'd like to do if I was no longer pack leader."

Allison snorted. "I'm not sure you know *how* to have a life anymore."

I bristled. I totally had a life. It might have been entrenched in violence, death, and way too many responsibilities, but I had a boyfriend and friends. The whole shebang. All I was missing was an occupation.

"We could go on a vacation," Chase suggested.

I looked at him like he was speaking in a foreign

tongue. "Vacation? What is this word? I'm not sure I've heard it before."

Chase laughed. "Don't worry. I'll teach you my ways."

"You guys better plan for Max and I to come along," Allison interjected.

"And me and . . . " Lucy trailed off. " . . . er, Lela."

Allison shoved Lucy's shoulder. "Don't worry, I'll find you a hot island man while we're on vacation."

I scoffed. "Who says we're going to an island? I want to go to the mountains."

Allison rolled her eyes. "We *live* in the mountains."

I glared at her. "This is why you're not invited."

"This is why I'm planning the entire thing," she countered.

I sighed and turned my gaze to Lucy. "When I give up pack responsibilities, can I give up Allison responsibilities too?"

"Only if Devin will take them," Lucy laughed. "That's *way* too much responsibility for me."

Allison crossed her arms and pouted, but I ignored it, finally feeling better. There was a light at the end of the tunnel. Maybe. I'd have to convince Devin first. I've been told I could be very persuasive, even when fireballs weren't involved. Maybe I'd butter him up with a road trip souvenir. Surely that would be enough to convince him to take on an entire werewolf pack. Right? Ri-ight.

# Chapter 6

Evening came far too quickly for my liking. The darkness pressed down on me like a heavy hand as we all made our way across the hotel parking lot. Alexius' leash was once again in my grasp, because I was afraid to leave him in the hotel room alone. It had initially seemed like a good idea to bring him on the road trip, but that was before murders and fires started happening. It might behoove me to pop him down to the demon world at some point to stay with Dorrie.

I patted Alexius on the head, then opened the vehicle door for him to climb inside, turning my thoughts to our mission. Abel was yet to find me any more information on Art, but maybe someone at the pack meeting would know something about him. Several of them had been his neighbors, after all.

The drive to our destination was short. I'd debated leaving Allison behind, but that would have left her unprotected in the hotel room. I wasn't sure if she was safer with us, or by herself, but at least this way I could run out to protect her. Yes, much to her chagrin, she'd be waiting in the car with Alexius. That way if someone tried to attack her, she could simply drive away. Lucy parked the car on the street in line with a few other vehicles.

I checked the scribbled address on the paper in my lap, just to be sure we had the right house. 102 Oakcrest drive seemed like a perfectly normal home in a perfectly normal neighborhood. The houses were obviously older, not the cookie-cutter structures of many newer subdivisions. The home we were expected at was expansive, probably five or six bedrooms all housed in a single story, making the house seem squat for how wide it was.

I gave Alexius a final pat, then opened the door. The cool night air filled my lungs as we exited the vehicle, leaving the dog safe within the car. I wasn't sure how he'd react to new werewolves, and I didn't really want to experiment.

I rubbed my arms to generate warmth as I glanced up at the moon. Only half full. *Good*. It was a bad idea to be around werewolves closer to the full moon. Most could control when they transformed, but they all seemed to get a little more . . . wolfy. Lucy included.

Lucy and I walked around the side of the car to meet Allison and Chase on the sidewalk. Lucy handed Allison the keys. We wanted her in the driver's seat and ready, just in case.

I rubbed my bare arms again. It was more chilly out than I'd expected. I wasn't used to the high desert norm of hot days and far cooler nights. I'd changed into jeans, but my simple white tee shirt left me with light goosebumps on my skin. It wasn't really *that* cold though. Maybe I was just nervous. Or maybe it was the energy from the nearby house filled with vampires and werewolves.

I stared at Allison until she met my eyes. "No getting out of the car, and keep the doors locked. If anyone bothers you, just drive away."

"Yes, mother," she replied sarcastically.

I sighed and glanced at the house. The wolves inside might not appreciate me bringing another demon along, but they were probably bringing vampires, so they couldn't really throw stones. Hopefully we'd be able to quickly explain that we'd had nothing to do with the fire and they'd let us go.

"Where's the *backup*?" Lucy asked nervously, glancing up and down the still street.

"There," Chase pointed.

I turned to see three shadowy figures walking across the road from us.

"Or else we're about to be attacked," Chase added.

I herded Allison behind me, envisioning a flame in my mind. I didn't form one in my hand, not yet, but I was ready.

"Ms. Meyers?" one of the figures questioned.

Oh good grief. "Call me Xoe," I sighed as the figures became clearly visible in front of us.

Our backup consisted of two men and a woman, appearing to be in their early twenties, or perhaps late teens. Abel had speculated before that younger wolves would be more apt to obey me. He was probably right. The men, one short and one tall, glanced at me nervously. They were dressed in typical young adult fashion, jeans and dark tee shirts with sneakers. Both had shaggy brown hair that fell into their eyes. I would have guessed they were brothers if not for the height difference. The woman eyed me apathetically. She had dark skin, short, curly black hair, and wore a jean jacket. She was the only one of us who'd been wise enough to bring a jacket, or maybe it was just a fashion statement. Her glaring eyes were accented with black liner, and gold jewelry sparkled at her neck and on her fingers. I was betting on fashion statement.

The shorter of the two men grinned at me. "Matt," he said pointing to himself, "Chris, and Jessica." He pointed to the other man and the woman respectively. "We're told you're in need of some back up."

"Let's hope not," I replied. "I'd like to be in and out of here as quickly as possible."

"Sounds good to me," the taller guy, Chris replied. "I have a hot date tonight."

"You do not," Jessica sighed, as if she'd heard the claim many times before.

Chris waggled his eyebrows at Allison. "Well I *could*," he hinted.

"No hitting on my friends," I ordered, bringing everyone's attention back to me.

Chris offered me a mock salute. "Yes, ma'm."

By his sarcastic mien, I was guessing he wasn't the one to call me *Ms. Meyers* when he first approached.

I glared at him. "I'd appreciate if you took this seriously. If any of my people get hurt tonight, I'll be coming after *you* for vengeance."

He smirked.

Yeah, definitely a problem.

"That's a lot of talk for such a willowy little girl."

Matt elbowed him in the ribs. "She's a pack leader, dude. Would you talk that way to Abel?"

"Go home," I ordered, giving Chris my best blank stare.

His expression softened in surprise. "I was only-"

"Go home," I said again. "I don't want someone like you at my back tonight."

He opened his mouth to argue as Matt and Jessica backed away from him, clearly distancing themselves. I continued to stare.

Seeing that no one was going to support him, his mouth set in a firm line. "I don't have to listen to you. We drove hours to get here, and they're my ride," he nodded in Jessica and Matt's direction.

I took a step forward. I considered summoning a fireball to scare him, but this guy was obviously all talk. He was a few inches taller than me, which made looking tough a little awkward. Good thing I'd had plenty of practice.

"*Look,*" I snapped. "Today is not my day. You're going to go back to the car you came here in and wait for your friends, or I'm going to take you to the demon underground and leave you there until we're done."

His eyes widened.

Mine didn't. I continued to stare him down.

"You would really do it, wouldn't you?" he questioned.

"Actually," Chase cut in, "you're quite lucky she didn't just throw a fireball at you. That's her usual method. She's playing nice right now."

Chris lifted his hands in surrender and backed away. "Fine. I guess all of the things I've heard about you are true. I'll wait in the car." He turned and walked away.

"Idiot," Jessica muttered at his back.

I raised an eyebrow at her, then moved my gaze to Allison.

"All right," she sighed, backing toward the car. "I'll be waiting to man the getaway vehicle."

I nodded, glanced in the direction Chris had gone to make sure he wasn't coming back, then led the way toward the house. Chris's little display of defiance had made us late.

"Yeah," Lucy muttered, reaching my side, "you *really* need a break from being pack leader."

"Aw," I joked, "and here I thought I was finally getting good at it."

She smirked. "That's kind of my point."

She was right. I was getting a little too good at it. A girl shouldn't boss werewolves around so easily. It was bad for ones health. Bossing Allison around was almost just as bad.

The front door opened before we reached it, revealing a tall man, somewhere in his late twenties. He was of Asian decent, and oozed enough power to draw goosebumps on my skin. "It's about time," he said in greeting, picking invisible lint off his black dress shirt and slacks. The formal wear seemed out of place with his black hair, short, but sticking out in all directions.

"Vampire," Lucy muttered, leaning toward my shoulder, though if the man really was a vampire, he'd hear us.

He smiled, showcasing little fangs. "Thanks for the introduction." He turned around and led the way into the house.

"Hi, nice to meet you," I muttered facetiously, "welcome to Spring Valley."

He glanced over his shoulder and raised an eyebrow at me, then turned forward and continued walking.

I followed, taking my time to observe our surroundings. The inside of the house seemed just as normal as the outside. Everyone followed us in. I heard the door shut behind us, but didn't bother to see who had shut it. I was too busy snooping.

The decor was pure, stereotypical middle American. Light colored wood furniture, probably made of particle board, adorned the empty living room. Beige carpeting accented matching overstuffed furniture and white walls.

We continued down the hall, decked with nondescript family photos, leaving the living room behind. A turn took us past the large kitchen, and down another hall.

The vampire stopped in front of a closed door in

the hallway and knocked.

Seconds later, the door opened from the inside, revealing an expansive room large enough to be a second living room, though the center was dominated by a large conference table instead of a sofa. Only half the seats were filled, but more people stood back along the far wall like good little bodyguards. They were all dressed like the vampire. Maybe he was a bodyguard too. Another black clad man, presumably the one that had opened the door, went to stand with everyone else.

Seated at the center of the table with her back turned to the people against the wall was a woman. Clearly the woman in charge. Black hair was cut into a sleek bob, framing a strong jaw and large, doe-like brown eyes. She sat with her fingers laced in front of her, smiling softly. What I could see of her clothing above the table was a fitted gray blazer and blue silk blouse.

We all stood awkwardly in the doorway. Our vampire escort had gone in, but hadn't motioned for us to follow.

"So," I began, "sorry about the fire, but it had nothing to do with me."

She smiled, though it seemed forced. "I don't care about the fire." She gestured to the empty seats at the table. "Please come in."

We did as we were asked, though everyone stayed a step behind me. None of us sat.

The woman's eyes flicked to those who'd accompanied me. "I'd hoped for less of an audience."

I raised an eyebrow at the people lined up against the wall behind her. "Get rid of some of yours, and maybe I'll ask some of mine to wait outside."

She seemed to deflate. She was nervous about something. Here I'd thought we were in for a lecture about a fire we hadn't caused. She gestured to the people lining the wall. They all moved away from their posts and toward us. We stepped out of the way, and they all went out into the hall and walked out of sight, save the vampire who'd led us in.

I found it odd that he'd be the one to stay rather than one of her wolves, but I didn't voice my concerns. We were no longer in a room full of unknown werewolves. The night was looking up.

"Your turn," she stated.

I turned and looked at Lucy, Matt, Jessica, and Chase. "Everyone but Chase, please go wait out in the hall."

Matt and Jessica seemed unsure of their duty, but finally nodded and left the room, followed by Lucy. Soon enough, Chase and I were alone in the room with the woman and her vampire bodyguard.

The woman looked Chase up and down, displaying increased anxiety. "I'd really rather not have any extra ears on this conversation."

I glanced at the closed door behind me, then back to her. "You do realize that all of those werewolves can probably hear us anywhere in the house, right?"

She rolled her eyes. "The room is soundproof. What we have to discuss requires privacy."

I nodded at the man standing behind her chair. "As long as your guard remains, so does mine." So Chase wasn't exactly my *guard*. She didn't need to know that.

She sighed and gestured for us to take a seat.

We did, at the opposite end of the table, out of reach.

"Straight to business then," she announced, "I have several missing wolves, and I need you to find them."

My eyes widened. "First, maybe you could start with an actual introduction. Second, I don't know what you've heard, but I'm not a detective."

"My name is Iva," she explained, then gestured to the vampire behind her. "This is Eric."

I waited for her to say more. She didn't. "Okay, Iva. Now tell me why you think I'm the person to find your missing wolves."

She glanced back to Eric, as if searching for reassurance. There was a softness in his gaze, causing me to suspect a less than professional relationship between the pair. Maybe even love. Eric nodded for her to continue.

She turned back to us. "Eric is skilled at finding information," she explained. "I know all about your role in taking down the witches that were kidnapping supernaturals last year, and I heard about you eliminating the rogue pack that wanted to defy the coalition."

I tried to keep the surprise off my face. It wouldn't be difficult to find out the information Eric had acquired, but if I took down that rogue pack, it was news to me. I'd been too busy dealing with my grandmother. All I'd done was talk to a few witches.

"I still don't understand why you're coming to me," I pressed. "Abel has far more resources for this type of thing."

She flinched.

Realization dawned on me. "Unless you haven't told Abel about any of this . . . "

She glanced at Eric again, then turned back to me and explained, "When the first two went missing, I thought I could handle it. It's my job to protect my pack, and I wanted to find them. Then more disappeared, and more time passed without me finding them. If I told him now, he'd probably kill me for not reporting it right away."

I stared at her, so surprised I had no idea what to say. I'd come for a lecture and was getting a plea for help instead. "Just how many wolves are missing now?"

She sighed. "Seven."

I pushed my chair out and stood abruptly. "No way. You need to tell Abel. He'll be able to find them much sooner than I could manage."

"If you want more information about your uncle," Eric said calmly, "I would sit down."

I met his dark, emotionless gaze. "Uncle?"

He nodded once. "Art."

That was news to me. Here I'd been thinking Art was maybe my third cousin twice removed, or something equally distant. Did that mean he was my grandmother Alexandria's son, just like my dad?

I sat back down. "I'm listening."

"He went missing around the same time as the first wolves," he explained. "I think the disappearances are connected."

I shook my head. "If that's the case, then your wolves are dead. I found Art's well-rotted corpse earlier today."

That seemed to give Eric pause. Goody.

"Be that as it may," he replied, seeming to recover, "I still know why Art was plotting against you."

It was my turn to be caught off guard. "How on earth would you know anything about that?"

"Finding information is what I do," he replied simply.

"Except you can't find seven missing wolves," I countered.

He frowned. "No, I cannot."

I turned back to Iva. "So you're proposing I find your wolves before Abel finds out, and you'll give me information about Art?"

She nodded once. "And money."

I shook my head. "No deal. I'll find information on my own. I won't tattle to Abel on you, but you better tell him yourself if you hope to find your people, alive or dead."

She stood, desperation contorting her face. "Please, he'll kill me," she begged.

I shook my head again. "Not my problem."

Chase, who'd been silent for the entire

conversation, grabbed my arm. "This may all be connected," he suggested. He glanced at Eric. "We could at least pool our resources and try to find Art's killer along with the missing wolves."

I tilted my head at him, digesting his point. I could admit that he had one. "Now why did you have to go and be all practical? I was about to make a dramatic exit."

I turned my gaze to Eric with narrowed eyes, considering the proposition. The wise thing to do would be to tell Abel right away and let him handle it. Unfortunately, few would call me wise. "I'm only in town until the end of the week. I'll help you until then, but I want that information regardless of whether or not we find the missing wolves." I moved my gaze to Iva. "*And*, if we can't find the missing wolves within that time frame, I want you to report it to Abel."

Iva rested her face in her palms, but eventually groaned, "Deal."

Eric nodded his assent, then moved to a file cabinet against one of the walls. He pulled a small ring of keys out of his pant pocket to unlock the top drawer, pulled out a manilla file folder, then shut the drawer and relocked it. He walked around the table and handed the file to me. "Here is information on each of the wolves, personal details, as well as where they were last seen, and by whom. I have a much thicker folder on Art, which I will relinquish at the end of the week, assuming you truly give this task your full effort."

I blinked up at him. "And why exactly do you have a thick file on a demon?"

He smirked. "He once tried to hire me to kill you."

"Oh?" I pressed, still gazing up at him.

"I refused," he stated simply.

"Because I'm just too sweet and adorable to kill?"

The smirk returned. "Something like that." He placed a business card on top of the envelope. "Call me if you find anything, or require any other assistance. I'm also aware that some of those accompanying you are from Abel's pack. I would appreciate it if you did not let them in on this case."

I gave him a mock salute, then looked down at the file curiously, wanting to open it, but not really desiring any more time around Eric. Iva still had her face buried in her palms, as if she knew her death was imminent. She might not be wrong.

I really didn't think Abel would kill her, but then again, what did I know? I was only familiar with the Abel that was old friends with my dad. Maybe he had a well-hidden dark side.

Didn't we all?

## Chapter 7

File in hand, we retreated with Lucy, Jessica, and Matt in tow. I didn't see any of Iva's other wolves as Eric escorted us out, but there were still plenty of cars parked in the street, leading me to believe they were somewhere else in the house. It wasn't any of my business though, and I didn't mind them not saying goodbye.

Eric left us at the door, and the five of us moved to stand beneath a streetlight. A moment later Allison hopped out of the car to join us, once again leaving Alexius inside. Poor boy. I really should have just left him in the demon underground where he'd be safe. I sighed at the thought. When the demon underground was safer than the human world, you knew you had problems. Big ones.

"Well thanks for joining us," I said, looking at Matt and Jessica. "Sorry there wasn't much use for you. Maybe we'll see you at the next coalition gathering."

Matt held up his hand to stop me. "Sorry, we're with you for the duration. At least until Abel is sure nobody is going to murder you like the other demon."

I narrowed my eyes at him. "So what, you're . . . bodyguards?"

He shrugged. "Actually we're college students, but we were the only ones available to send since we're all on Spring Break." He looked to Jessica. "Though *some* of us would have preferred to remain by a nice swimming pool for the duration."

I sighed. "I'm guessing I don't have the power to counteract Abel's direct orders?"

"Nope," he replied. "We are to obey you, but not if you tell us to leave."

I snorted. "Abel said that specifically, didn't he."

Matt grinned. "He seemed to think you'd try to send us away the first chance you got. He was basically right."

I turned at the sound of footsteps to see Chris trotting across the dark street. I wanted to argue, but I was also tired, and dying to look at the file away from prying eyes. "We're staying at the *Gentle View Hotel*," I conceded.

Matt rocked back and forth on his feet, from heel to toe, with his hands in his pockets. "I know. We stopped and got a room on our way here."

If I kept sighing I was eventually going to hyperventilate. "Lovely," I grumbled. "I imagine we'll see you there."

"You imagine correctly," he said with a wink.

"Whatever," Jessica grumbled, rolling her eyes at Matt. "Can we go?"

"Yes, please," Chris growled, remaining in the shadows.

With a wave from Matt, they departed back in

the direction Chris had come from.

"What a cheery bunch," Chase observed. "At least they procured their own room."

I glanced down at the file in my hand. "Yeah," I muttered, "at least there's that. Let's go."

As we moved toward the car, Lucy asked, "Is anybody going to tell me what the file folder is for?"

"Shh," I whispered, not sure if Abel's wolves had gone out of hearing range.

She promptly obeyed.

Not asking questions, Allison climbed back into the driver's seat. Chase and I resumed our seats in the back with welcoming kisses from Alexius. Lucy got in last as Allison started the engine, flipped on the lights, then pulled out onto the dark street. The car's dash flashed 11:30. Lovely. It was going to be a late night if I planned on going through the entire folder, which I did.

Chase glanced down at the folder in my lap expectantly.

I shrugged. May as well start now.

Lucy turned in her seat as I flipped on the dome light. "*Now* will you tell me what's in the folder?"

"Information on seven wolves," I explained, peering down at the first page. "All missing."

"Does Abel know?" she questioned.

"Nope," I replied. "And we're not telling him until the end of the week. Not if we want bountiful information on Art. Iva, the pack leader, wants to find out what happened to them before Abel catches wind of the situation."

Lucy turned back around in her seat and sighed. "I wish you wouldn't have told me that."

I lifted my gaze from the paper. "What? Why?"

She turned around again. Her face held concern. "Because I'm just a lowly pack member, and my Alpha is asking me to keep information from the coalition leader."

"But I'm making you," I countered. "Doesn't that mean that only I will get in trouble?"

"Not necessarily," she groaned.

Suddenly suspicious, I asked. "Have you gotten in trouble with Abel before?"

She shook her head. "No, but Lela got in big trouble after the whole Dan incident."

My eyes widened. "But Dan was murderous and psychotic, and also dealing with demons. He *forced* Lela to follow him. It wasn't her choice."

Lucy rolled her eyes at me. "There's *always* a choice."

That gave me pause. Lucy *was* making a choice. She had the option of reporting me to Abel for keeping Iva's secret. I really didn't think Abel would punish Lucy for something I made her do, but I wasn't entirely sure. I wasn't willing to risk it.

"Maybe we should just tell Abel about the missing wolves then," I sighed. "We can still look for information on Art on our own. There's no guarantee they even have anything we don't already know."

"I'm guessing Iva knows just what will happen to her if Abel finds out?" Lucy questioned.

I nodded. "She seemed to think he'd kill her, but

I don't know. All of this pack law stuff is still mostly beyond me. It seems a harsh punishment for the alleged crime."

Lucy raised an eyebrow at me. "If she would have reported it right away, Abel could have used his influence to find the missing wolves. Now they might be dead because what, she was too prideful to ask for help?"

I frowned. Another good point. "Something like that. She wanted to protect her pack on her own. She seemed to think Eric would be able to find them no problem."

"Eric?" Lucy questioned.

"The vampire," I explained. "He's apparently quite adept at gathering information. He claims to have an entire file on Art. He also claimed Art tried to hire him to kill me."

Lucy gasped. "He tried to put a hit out on you?"

I nodded.

"What if Art had hired someone else, and that someone doesn't know that Art is dead?" she blurted. "There could be a supernatural assassin after you right this moment."

I pursed my lips as a thought came to me. "Or else the assassin turned on Art, and that's how he ended up dead."

"It's not worth risking," Lucy countered. "We need that information, and we need to ask Eric if anyone else was hired after him."

I shook my head. "We need to tell Abel what's going on so you don't get in trouble."

"Absolutely not," Lucy snapped. "I can handle a little bit of punishment, if it even comes to that. I'm not going to let information go when people are trying to *kill* you."

I sighed and leaned my head back against my seat. "People are *always* trying to kill me."

"Not vampire assassins," she argued.

I rolled my eyes at her. "We don't even know if Eric is an actual assassin. Maybe Art was just desperate and reached out to him."

Lucy eyed me, her lips set in a firm line. "We're not taking that risk. We'll try to find the missing wolves this week. If we don't find them, do we still get the information on Art?"

I nodded.

"Good," she replied. "For now, we'll watch our backs, and hopefully we can get to the bottom of this. We'll need to call Sam. See if he's heard anything about assassins or the missing wolves."

I stared at her like she'd grown a second head.

She paused, then asked, "What?"

I shook my head and laughed. "Maybe *you* should be the new pack leader."

She snorted. "I'm not alpha enough, and I'd rather focus on school. Devin is the better choice."

I gave her a little salute. "Ma'm, yes Ma'm."

We didn't have time to say more as Allison pulled the car into the hotel parking lot. Jessica, Chris, and Matt all waited outside a small white sedan, parked in the spot we'd previously vacated. Allison maneuvered the car to park next to them.

I stepped out of the car to stand in front of the trio, tugging Alexius out behind me. "I thought you said you had a room."

Matt glanced down at Alexius, but didn't comment on his presence. "Just wanted to make sure you got back safe," he explained. "Also," he typed something into a cell phone in his hand, then looked back up at me, "I just sent you a text with all our numbers."

I bit my lip to hide my irritation. Did Abel really have to go around handing out my cell number to people? If I really did step down as pack leader, I'd have to change my number to filter out the calls.

"Great," I replied as my phone buzzed in my pocket. I gave the three of them a little wave. "I'm going to bed now."

Matt waved cheerfully while the other two just rolled their eyes.

"Lets go," I grumbled to my friends as the other wolves walked away.

I clutched the file folder against my chest while Lucy led the way toward the stairs. Alexius trotted happily beside me, glad to be out of the car. I glanced at Chase as he walked by my other side, lingering on his scrunched brow and pensive expression.

"Thinking about assassins?" I asked.

He glanced at me, now smiling softly. "Do you blame me?"

I shook my head. "No, but no one has tried to kill me since I came back from the dead. I think we're okay." I laughed. "And even if I die, maybe the vampire blood will bring me back."

Chase stumbled in front of the stairs. He stopped to glare at me. "I'm pretty sure it's out of your system by now."

"Unless I'm a half-vampire and don't even know it," I sniped. So maybe I was still a little bitter about it.

"You're not a vampire," Allison cut in, moving past us to ascend the stairs. "You would have eaten me by now. I'm sure my blood is quite exquisite."

"Let's cut you open and try some," I replied, following her up with Alexius in tow.

We reached the door to our room.

Allison inserted the key card and grinned at me. "You better be careful with your jokes or I won't invite you over the threshold. You'll have to sleep on the balcony."

She opened the door and I strode past her into the room. "That's it. I'm definitely going to bite you now."

Everyone followed me inside. The bed looked incredibly appealing, but I knew I wouldn't be lying in it anytime soon. I glanced down at the folder in my hand as the door shut behind Chase, then settled for sitting on the foot of the bed to peruse it. Alexius hopped up and snuggled near the pillows, as if mocking me.

As soon as Chase sat beside me, I looked over at him expectantly. "We should probably call Sam sooner rather than later to see if he can find any information. The sooner we figure this mystery out, the better."

He nodded and silently retrieved his phone from his pocket.

I noticed Lucy watching us from the other bed as Chase scanned his contacts for Sam's number, even though Allison had the TV back on in front of them. I'd suspected before that she might have a bit of a crush on Sam, but I hoped I was wrong. He may have been useful, but he was also bad news. I'd have to needle her about it later.

I shook my head and looked back down at the file as Chase stood and walked further away from the TV to speak with Sam. From what I had gathered in my preliminary glances, the wolves had nothing in common except for being part of the same pack. Three were younger, four older. Five females and two males. Occupations ranging from waitress to lawyer. I had no idea where to even start, so I studied the photos stapled to each sheet of information. Figuring I should review the photos often to memorize the faces, I pulled out my phone and took a picture of each. That way if we happened upon one of them, I'd be able to verify by appearance. While I was at it, I went back to Eric's card and entered his number into my phone, just in case something happened and I lost the information.

After a hushed phone call, Chase came to stand before me, a chagrinned expression on his face.

I raised an eyebrow at him.

"He's coming here," he explained.

I groaned. I did *not* want to deal with Sam

tonight.

Lucy once again flicked her gaze to us. "Why is he coming here? We need him to ask around the underground for information."

Chase's chagrined expression deepened. "He claimed he simply couldn't miss out on an adventure where assassins are involved."

I groaned again. "We don't even know that assassins are involved. Call him back and tell him we probably won't be risking life and limb at all."

An eerie feeling pervaded the atmosphere. Chase sighed. "Too late."

I recognized the odd feeling, akin to standing in the middle of a graveyard. *Ghosts.* Gre-at. A second later there was a knock on the door.

"Maybe we shouldn't answer it," I suggested.

Chase moved toward the door, shoulders slumped in defeat. "He's been able to track me with ease ever since I started sensing ghosts," he explained. "He knows we're in here."

He opened the door to reveal Sam, standing out in the darkness. Even after the time we'd spent together, I was still always taken aback by how much Sam and Chase looked alike. Sam was several inches shorter, his jaw a little more square, but they were clearly brothers. Sam wore all black to match his hair and accent his dark gray eyes, the same shade as Chase's.

"I hear we're looking for kidnapped werewolves and perhaps an assassin or two," he said upon entering the room.

Allison scoffed and rolled her eyes at him.

Lucy pawed nervously at her hair.

"Yes," I answered, rising from the bed, "and we were hoping you could look for information . . . underground."

He raised a dark brow at me as Chase shut the door behind him. "Now what sense would it make for me to look around from down there? My guess is your missing wolves aren't in the demon city." He paused and glanced around at everyone staring at him. "They aren't, are they?"

I clenched my jaw in irritation, then resigned myself. He was right. He was probably more useful to us here. I turned toward the bed and shuffled the papers back into the folder, then handed it to him. "Acquaint yourself."

He looked down at the folder, then up to me. "I thought we could just go look at your murdered uncle then go from there."

I looked past him to Chase. "Was it necessary to tell him *everything*?"

Chase shrugged as Lucy asked, "Uncle?"

I glanced over my shoulder to explain, "Art. He was my uncle . . . allegedly."

Her mouth formed a soft *'oh'* of understanding.

I turned around and offered the folder once more to Sam. "If you're going to actually be useful, you should at least know what the missing wolves look like."

He sighed and took the folder, then walked past me to sit on the bed beside Lucy, muttering something like, "I'm *always* useful."

Lucy stiffened as soon as he sat, and suddenly seemed at a loss as to what to do with herself. Funny that the most capable person in our group was so horribly nervous around boys she liked.

Sam flipped through the pages one by one while we all waited. As he reached the last he looked up at me. "Am I supposed to find anything out of the ordinary in here?"

I shook my head. "Not unless you're far more observant than I. As far as I could tell, there's no link between any of them, except that they're all members of the same pack."

"So someone targeting the pack as a whole," Sam deduced.

I nodded, then resumed my seat on the bed opposite Sam, Lucy, and Allison. "I figured we'd start in the morning by questioning the other pack members. We'll speak with the last people to see them, and maybe visit the places they were taken from. I'll be counting on your ghosts to spot anything mortal eyes might overlook, and I was also hoping you could try contacting Art's ghost, just in case it's still hanging around."

He glanced past me at Chase, who still stood by the foot of the bed, then returned his gaze to me. "You know your boyfriend over there can do all of the stuff you're asking for, right?"

I turned my gaze to Chase as he moved to sit beside me. I knew he could *see* ghosts, but I wasn't aware of how far his powers had come. "Is this true?"

I questioned. I almost felt bad for asking since he never seemed to want to talk about his powers, nor had he offered to demonstrate them, but it felt odd that I didn't know.

He cringed. "Yeah, though I'm not really adept at *using* them as much as he is." He nodded in Sam's direction.

I frowned, but accepted his answer. I could always grill him for more details later.

"I'll search for your uncle's ghost," Sam acquiesced, "but don't get your hopes up."

Lucy cleared her throat, then blushed when Sam looked at her. "There's just one problem. How are we going to do all of this investigating with Abel's people following our every move?"

I thought about it for a moment, then lifted a finger in the air as a lightning bolt hit me. I moved the finger to point in Lucy and Allison's direction. "You two can take them to dig up more information on Art under the pretense that we'll get more done if we split up into groups. That will leave Chase, Sam, and I free to investigate the missing wolves without anyone reporting back to Abel."

Allison tilted her head in thought. "So we'd basically be leading them on a wild goose chase to keep them busy while you snoop about?"

I shrugged. "Or you might actually find some information on Art. Either way, it will help our cause."

Allison smirked. "Sounds fun enough. I'm in."

Lucy looked like she wanted to protest, but

didn't say anything.

"What about Nix?" Chase questioned.

Sam's eyes widened. "The crazy chick that came with us to the dream realm?"

I bit my lip. Had I really seen her? I wasn't sure. "I thought maybe I saw her earlier today, but it was just a glimpse. It could have been anyone watching us."

"Do you think your ghosts could track her if she really has returned to the human world?" I asked.

Sam inclined his head. "They can try, though she's a slippery one."

I nodded. "Trying is good enough. It probably wasn't her, but if it was, I want to know. I have no desire to relive my first encounter with her."

"Done," he replied.

We all nodded, our plans settled.

When Sam remained seated on the bed, I eyed him expectantly.

"What?" he questioned.

"It's late," I explained. "Some of us aren't partially nocturnal."

He glanced up toward the pillows on the bed, then turned back to look at Lucy and Allison. "I'm pretty sure we could all fit. We'd just have to squeeze in *real* tight."

Allison snorted in reply. Lucy didn't comment.

I stood, then grabbed his arm to haul him off the bed. "We'll see you in the morning," I said tiredly. "If you'd like it to be a pleasant day, bring coffee. Oh," I added, letting go of Sam to tug Alexius' collar to remove him from the bed. "And take Alexius to Dorrie. I don't want him getting caught in any of the crossfire."

Sam crouched down to pet Alexius, who seemed to like him. Imagine that. Here I thought dogs were a good judge of character. Sam kept one hand on Alexius and gave me a mock salute with the other before shadowy figures enveloped him. As he began to fade from sight, he cheerfully said, "Aye aye, captain."

I started to reach out to stop him. I hadn't expected him to leave so easily, and hadn't said goodbye to Alexius, but I was too late. They had both disappeared.

"Tomorrow is going to be a long day," I whined, resuming my seat on the bed.

Chase wrapped an arm around my shoulders. "Try being *his* brother."

I turned to eye him seriously. "You make me very glad to be an only child."

"He's not *that* bad," Lucy muttered.

I reached to the top of the bed, then threw a pillow at her. "You only think that because you're in *lo-ove* with him."

She caught the pillow and crushed it against her lap. "I am not!" she argued, her face beet red.

I rolled my eyes, then said jokingly to Chase, "You should have *seen* the hard time these two gave me when they were forcing me to admit my feelings for you." I turned back to Lucy. "It's only fair that I get to do the torturing this time."

"I am *not* interested in him," she said more firmly.

I chuckled, then rose from the bed to search my duffel bag for pajamas. "*Please.* You're forgetting that I'm the queen of denial. It enables me to spot it a mile away."

Lucy blushed harder, but didn't argue.

"Hey," I said, tapping her arm as I walked past her on my way to the bathroom. "Don't feel bad. Sam may be a pest," I glanced back at Chase, then back to her, "but he has good genes."

She continued to glare at me, though there was a hint of a smile on her lips. She would forgive me for the teasing. That's what best friends are for.

That, and distracting three nosy werewolves from interfering with my paranormal investigation.

# Chapter 8

A knock on the door woke me. I turned and wiggled loose from the circle of Chase's arms to glance at the bedside clock. 7:30 am. What unholy monster was awaking us at 7:30 am?

When no one else so much as twitched, I forced myself out of bed and placed my bare feet on the floor to stand. I grabbed my phone from the beside table out of habit, then winced when I saw a text from Jason. I'd forgotten to text him the previous night to let him know we were all still alive.

I stood and made my way to the door, muttering curses under my breath. I'd call Jason as soon as I had a moment. The door's peephole revealed Sam, carrying a cardboard drink carrier with four cups of coffee, and a fifth in his free hand.

I opened the door. "Early," I stated.

He lips tilted into a crooked half smile. "Yes it is."

I looked down at his hands. "Coffee."

"Yep." He handed me the drink carrier and I turned away. "One of them is decaf," he explained to my back. "I figured you could have fun guessing which one."

I glared over my shoulder at him. "*Death*."

"Oh come now," he said good-naturedly, stepping inside to shut the door behind him.

Everyone else was finally getting out of bed as the smell of coffee seeped into the room. I looked down at the coffees, wondering if one really was decaf.

"They're all caffeinated," Sam whispered as he strolled past me, his own cup in hand. "I know not to risk death so early in the morning."

I took one of the coffees out of the tray, then handed the rest to Chase as he moved to stand beside me. I held the paper cup up to my face, inhaling the aroma through the plastic lid. I instantly felt less annoyed. Really, back when I'd been learning to control my temper to keep from setting things on fire, my friends should have just kept coffee nearby at all times. It soothed me like nothing else could.

I turned my gaze to Chase as I took my first sip. His black hair was rumpled from sleep, sticking out in all directions. His plaid pajama pants were one of the only pairs he owned. He'd worn them regularly on Sundays, our lazy, wear pajamas all day movie day. Having retrieved his coffee from the holder, he held out the last two cups to Allison as she approached.

She looked just as rumpled as Chase did, and twice as cranky as I felt. She'd never been a morning person. One of our few shared traits.

Lucy quickly did her best to straighten her hair before taking her offered coffee from Allison.

I knew I should get dressed and get on with the day, but figured a few cozy coffee moments couldn't hurt. I sat back down on mine and Chase's bed, while Sam resumed his seat from the previous night next to Lucy.

"I did a little bit of investigating last night," he began.

"Don't you sleep?" I interrupted.

He smirked. "Rarely. As I was saying, I did some investigating hoping to dig up a little bit of info on what we're dealing with. There haven't been any reported disappearances anywhere else in the supernatural community, so I think this is isolated to Spring Valley, and to the local werewolf pack specifically. I haven't found any information that would suggest Art's death is in any way linked. Now, if we find any of the wolves with matching daggers sticking out of them, then we can alter that assertion. Finally, I was not able to find any sign of Art's ghost, though I had little to go on in tracking him, so that's not saying much. Most likely, he's already moved on."

I took another sip of my coffee as my half-asleep brain sifted through everything he'd said. I didn't have high hopes in tracking Art's ghost, but hearing the news that Sam couldn't find him was still a letdown. "Any idea where we should start looking for the wolves then?"

He shrugged noncommittally. "Honestly, I'd start with the pack leader. She's their connection. This may all be because someone has a vendetta against her."

I nodded. "Maybe I'll call Eric, her pet vampire.

He said he'd give me any more information I might need."

Chase made a *hmph* sound. "He seemed like he would be loyal to her, and probably won't let anything slip if she's to blame. Though you never know. Perhaps it was all an act for her benefit."

I nodded. "It's worth a shot, at least." I shifted my gaze to Lucy and Allison. "Maybe you guys can snoop around the RV park? See if there's any evidence remaining? That ought to give the rest of us at least an hour or two to speak with Eric."

"If we can even convince Abel's people to come with us instead of you," Lucy muttered.

I sighed. "Yeah, that might be a problem. We'll just have to do our best. Although speaking of them, I'm surprised Matt hasn't come to bug us yet."

I retrieved my cellphone from the night stand and searched for the text he'd sent me last night, then dialed the number. Everyone waited while I held the phone to my ear. A moment later, I lowered it. "Straight to voicemail," I explained before dialing one of the two numbers he'd sent me, either Jessica's or Chris'. Hopefully Jessica's.

Another voicemail. I dialed the third number. It just continued to ring until telling me the user was yet to set up their voice mailbox. "We'll that's portentous."

Lucy's eyes widened. "No answer from any of them?"

I shook my head. "Did anyone see what room they went to?"

Lucy stood. "I did. I'll go check."

"Take Sam with you," I advised before really thinking about it. He could at least transport her away from any danger with her ghosts, but I didn't necessarily trust him to do so.

Allison stood beside Lucy. "I'll go too."

Sam didn't speak. He simply stood and followed Lucy and Allison to the door. A moment later, it shut behind them.

Once we were alone, I turned to Chase. "I don't like this. Not one bit."

He nodded, looking down at the forgotten cup of coffee in his hand, then back to me. "If they're missing we'll have to tell Abel, and that will lead us to divulging everything about Iva's missing wolves."

"I know, but let's wait to see if they're actually missing first."

My phone buzzed in my lap. Maybe it was one of them calling me back. I lifted it to see Devin's number and felt suddenly nervous. Had Abel already somehow divined that his people were missing? Maybe he'd tried to call them for a status update.

"Hello?" I answered, lifting the phone to my ear.

"Xoe," Devin breathed. "Thank goodness you answered."

My heart stopped. "What is it? Did something happen in Shelby? Is it Emma's father?"

"No," he replied quickly, "but I think something has happened to Abel. He had finished up his pressing business and was on his way to meet you in Spring

Valley. He left late last night, and had promised me a status update as soon as he reached you. He should have been there by now. I called Darla. She hasn't heard from him."

My heart was thudding in my chest. Darla was Abel's wife, so it was a bad sign she hadn't heard from him. Maybe he had just stopped to rest, but I doubted it. Lucy, Allison, and Sam chose that moment to return.

"They're gone," Lucy said, "and their room is trashed."

"Xoe?" Devin's voice called in my ear. "What's going on there?"

I nodded to Lucy, then turned my back on her to focus on the phone call. "Devin, I think we have a problem. A big one."

I wanted to keep Iva's secret to gain information on Art, but it would be way too selfish to do it now. Too many people were missing. If Abel and the others showed up suddenly unharmed, I'd feel stupid, but stupid was better than dealing with the possibility of everyone being dead by the time we found them. If they weren't already.

I explained everything to Devin, including the meeting with Iva and the few things I'd learned about Art.

He was silent for several seconds, then said. "I'm coming down there."

"What about the rest of the pack?" I questioned instantly. "We can't just leave Emma and Siobhan to fend for themselves."

"I'll bring everyone with me."

"But then you'll risk all of them being taken too!"

He was silent for several more seconds. "I'll call for reinforcements here, then Jason and I will come down."

I paused while I thought about his offer. It seemed like a good compromise. I didn't want to endanger Devin or Jason, but I was also acutely aware of the risks the rest of us would be taking working with such a small group. "How soon can you be here?"

"As soon as reinforcements are arranged, we'll catch the first flight down, unless . . . "

I resisted slapping my palm against my face as I realized I was being silly. I could *travel*, so I could go and grab each of them one at a time. Now that I'd been to Spring Valley, I would be able to return. I didn't like leaving everyone else alone for even a second, but it would be safer for all if we got Devin and Jason down here sooner rather than later.

"Let me know once you have reinforcements and I'll come get you."

"Okay," Devin agreed. "You should probably remain hidden in the meantime. Matt, Jessica, and Chris definitely aren't the strongest wolves around, but to have three of them taken at once means we're dealing with a group effort."

I bit my lip. He was probably right, but . . . "I was going to call Eric, the vampire with all the info to see what I can get out of him. Iva should probably know too."

"Unless they're behind this."

I inhaled sharply. I hadn't even thought about that, and it was stupid of me not to. What if Iva had gone rogue, and hoped to take down the coalition? The missing wolves could all be part of her scheme to lure Abel and I in. Everyone knew that he'd given me his protection. If I was in danger, he would come.

"This is *not* good," I muttered.

"I know," Devin replied. "You should probably change hotels just to be safe. Tell no one where you're staying, and I'll contact you as soon as possible."

I nodded, then realizing he couldn't see it, I sighed. "You know I hate hiding, but I think you're right."

"Wow," he mumbled.

"What?"

"I was just shocked that you're actually listening to me. Find a new hideout then sit tight. I'll be in touch soon. "

Before I could comment he hung up. I lowered the phone to my lap, feeling stunned. I looked over my shoulder to find everyone staring at me. Lucy had probably heard the other half of the conversation with her werewolf hearing, but for everyone else's benefit I explained, "We think Abel is missing too. We need to find a new place to hide out, then I'll go and fetch Devin and Jason. Devin is calling in reinforcements to watch over Emma and the others while he's away."

"Maybe we should leave Spring Valley altogether," Sam suggested. "I'm not keen on the idea of going up against someone who can make so many wolves vanish without a trace."

"I'm not going to just abandon them," I snapped. "I may not be Abel's biggest fan, but if I was missing, he'd look for me. I at least owe him the same in return."

Sam lifted his hands in surrender. "Calm down, just a suggestion. No reason to throw any fireballs or anything."

I slumped, feeling suddenly defeated, then leaned my shoulder against Chase's. After a brief reprieve, I stood. "We need to get dressed, pack our stuff, and get out of here. If someone took the other wolves from their room, they probably know we're staying here." I glanced at Allison. "I can take you back to Shelby when I go to pick up Devin," I added.

She crossed her arms and pursed her lips, letting me know what she was going to say before she said it. "I'm not going anywhere."

I leveled my gaze at her. "We might not be able to protect you while we're defending ourselves."

"I can protect myself."

I raised an eyebrow at her. "Against someone or something that can kidnap werewolves?"

She snorted. "I've done it before."

"Fine," I snapped. "But if it looks like there's going to be a confrontation. I want you to run the other way and hide. Only fight if you have no choice."

"Fine."

I moved toward my suitcase to find some clothes to wear. I would have liked a shower, but I suddenly didn't feel at all safe in the hotel room. We needed a better place to hide, and despite what Devin had said, I needed to talk to Eric, *alone*. If he and Iva were truly behind everything, I'd go directly to the source.

I pawed through my clothing until I found something fitting my mood, all black, of course. Low-heeled black boots would complete the outfit. Screw the heat. Clothes in hand, I turned to look at everyone in the room. I didn't like endangering any of them, even Sam, but at least he and I could transport ourselves out of danger if we were taken like the others. Chase, Lucy, and Allison wouldn't be so lucky. That though alone made me want to send them all home, but I knew they wouldn't leave willingly. Especially Chase.

He eyed me with cold determination, and I knew for a fact he was trying to think of some way to send *me* home, or at least to the demon underground where vampires and werewolves couldn't reach me.

I let out a shaky breath and made my way into the bathroom to change and brush my teeth, wishing my dad were alive, or at the very least, that Abel would show up. Abel was far more well-equipped to handle things like this than I was. He had connections, and knew how to get information. I was just flying blind.

Fortunately flying blind is my specialty, but some things were beyond escaping by the skin of your teeth. Some things needed a plan. Damned if I knew what ours was.

## Chapter 9

Once we were all dressed and ready to go, we decided to take a quick look at the room where the other wolves had been taken. I doubted we'd find much evidence, but as soon as the cleaning staff happened upon the scene, it would be reported to the police, and we'd have no chance of going back to look.

The hotel room door had been left slightly ajar, bumping up against a piece of torn up carpeting. With everyone standing behind me, I gave the door a gentle push. Since Lucy, Allison, and Sam had already checked the room, I knew there likely wasn't anyone waiting inside to attack me, but I still took a defensive step back as the door swung inward.

They'd said the room was trashed, but I wouldn't say that was the correct term. Utterly obliterated, maybe. It looked like the beds and pillows had been stabbed. The furniture shattered into splinters. How other guests hadn't heard anything was beyond me. Unless they had and the police were just taking their sweet time coming to investigate.

I doubted we'd find any clues in the chaos, but it was worth a shot. I nodded to Sam and Allison as I went in, followed only by Chase and Lucy. The other two would stand guard in case anyone approached. I had no desire to get caught snooping about the destroyed room. I had enough problems as it was.

I tiptoed around the room, fighting down my anxiety to a manageable level. I started with the beds while Chase went to check the bathroom. Lucy sniffed around the room for any clue about the intruders, but since it was a hotel room, she might just end up scenting the cleaning staff or previous guests.

I lifted one of the tattered comforters to better observe the bed. Not knife damage after all, or at least not like any knife I'd ever seen. It was like something had suctioned the mattress with enough force to pull the springs and stuffing through the fabric, only to let go, dropping the tattered bedding back down on top of it.

I glanced around the rest of the room, imagining the same thing. Curious, I looked up at the ceiling as Lucy came to stand beside me.

She looked up too. "Damaging the ceiling seems a little excessive," she commented.

I shook my head as Chase returned to us. "The damage wasn't on purpose. Or at least, if I would have done it, it wouldn't have been on purpose."

I looked back down to meet Chase's questioning gaze.

I took a deep breath and glanced up at the ceiling again. "This room looks exactly how it would if I'd made a portal in it. Like everything has been lifted by the force of the propulsion, only to drop back down once the portal closed."

Chase and Lucy both looked at me wide eyed.

"But aren't you the only demon capable of making portals?" Lucy asked quietly.

"Yeah," I mumbled. "Or so I thought. Let's get out of here."

Chase nodded. "Good idea."

We met the others out on the balcony, then hustled everyone down toward Allison's car. I explained my theory as we went.

Sam seemed confused. "If any other demons could make portals, I would have heard of it."

Allison trotted to catch up to my side. "What if it's someone trying to frame you?"

I stopped walking, considering the thought. The sun beat down on my face, making me feel overheated, or maybe it was just from the sliver of panic in my gut. "But for what purpose?" I asked finally. "The coalition is responsible for maintaining paranormal law. The person that would investigate my possible involvement is Abel."

Lucy shook her head, moving to stand on my other side. "But Abel is missing, which means someone else will have to take over in his stead. Maybe that person is behind all of this. They could take over the coalition, and use you as a scape goat."

My head was spinning. It was far-fetched, but still a possibility. I needed to call Devin and figure out who would take over should Abel perish.

"Let's get out of here before we discuss it further," I advised.

We all piled into the car with Lucy and Allison

in front, and the rest of us in the back. I got stuck in the middle seat, even though I needed just as much leg room as Sam. The discomfort, however, was the last thing on my mind. If this wasn't all some sort of set up, then there was another demon capable of making portals. If this *was* a set up, I hated to even think about the implications. I almost hoped it was another demon.

Chase seemed deep in thought as we left the hotel parking lot.

I eyed him, but he didn't seem to notice. "Penny for your thoughts?"

He glanced at me and frowned. "I was just thinking about Nix. Portals are needed to travel to and from the dream realm. If you really did spot her yesterday, then that would support the theory of another portal making demon."

"Someone could have summoned her out," Sam countered.

"But who?" Chase asked. "She had no idea we were going to the dream world when she jumped us, and as far as we knew, she was a fugitive working alone, stuck in the human world. Who would have been in place to summon her out? It seems just as likely that another portal-making demon found her there, and brought her back to the mortal realm."

I leaned back against my seat in thought. "You know, *we* could try summoning her. Maybe she'll tell us how she got out."

Chase seemed to consider it. "But Cynthia and Rose are in Shelby, and we don't know any other witches."

Lucy turned around in her seat to involve herself in the conversation. "Abel would be able to locate witches to help us."

I took a steadying breath. "Yes, but we have to do this without Abel. If we end up with only dead ends, we'll go back to Shelby and convince Rose and Cynthia to help us."

Sam chuckled. "They weren't too thrilled last time you made them summon demons."

Chase cleared his throat. "And the demon you'd be asking them to summon murdered Cynthia's husband and other daughter."

I shook my head. I knew Cynthia would be against it, but, "If Nix really is back in the human world, it would be in Cynthia's best interest to help us get rid of her."

Sam tsked at us. "Or else we'll be summoning her out of the dream realm and therefore putting the witches in danger they could have otherwise avoided."

Allison glanced back over her shoulder as she hit a red light. "Mind telling me where we're going? Another hotel?"

I bit my lip in thought. Whoever had taken the other wolves had found our hotel easy enough, yet they hadn't bothered to target the rest of us. It made the possibility of me being framed more likely. Why take out three of Abel's unsuspecting minions and not the rest of us?

"Another hotel, I guess," I replied. "I don't know where *else* we would go. Then we need to talk to Eric. Find out what he knows."

"But what if he's behind this?" Lucy questioned.

I pursed my lips. "Maybe we can follow him."

Sam and Chase both raised their eyebrows at me in identical expressions. "Follow a vampire?" Sam asked. "Good luck."

"Jason is coming down with Devin," I explained. "Maybe he'll know how to follow Eric without him noticing. He might even *know* Eric. There aren't that many vampires in existence, and most seem to know each other."

"It's a good place to start," Chase agreed, not commenting on how he felt about my ex boyfriend coming down to help us.

Probably not as nervous as me. I wasn't worried about the two of them fighting, but they had banded together to slip me the vampire blood. I really didn't need them devising any more plots to ensure my longevity.

"Err," Allison interrupted. "Is that smoke?"

We all turned to see where she was pointing as she drove. It did look like smoke. A lot of it.

I groaned. "What are the chances it has something to do with us?"

"Ninety-nine out of one hundred," Lucy sighed.

"Should we check it out?" Allison asked, already turning the car in the general direction of the smoke.

I remained silent as we drove. Black plumes poured upward into the sky. It looked like it was coming from a residential area, so a house fire, or maybe another RV park. They were a plentiful occurrence in Spring Valley, as were fires, apparently.

"What if it's a trap to lure us in?" Sam questioned.

"We won't get out of the car," I muttered.

Allison drove the car closer to the source of the smoke, though we had to pull over once for fire trucks to pass us by. My eyes scanned the buildings and sidewalks bordering the street. I kept expecting to see Nix pop out at any minute, though we weren't all that near the fire yet.

We slowed as we reached a neighborhood street that seemed about right to lead to the fire. The other clue was the police car blocking off entry. Allison continued driving to the next street, also blocked, this time by a large sign spanning across the center of the road.

"If we want to get a closer look, we'll have to get out and walk," Chase commented, looking past me at the next blocked street.

"Trap, party of five?" Sam muttered sarcastically.

Allison pulled the car up a little further to park on the side of the street, just past the second road block sign.

Sam turned his eyes to me. "I thought you said we wouldn't get out of the car."

I waved him off as Allison shut off the engine.

We all got out.

"Are they always this great at listening?" Sam

asked Lucy as Chase, Allison, and I walked around from our side of the car.

I reached her side in time to see her smirk. "They only ignore voices of reason. Start suggesting dangerous, unreasonable schemes and they'll be all ears."

"Hey I listen," I argued, then shrugged, "then sometimes I do what I was going to do anyway, but I still *listen*."

"I rest my case," Lucy muttered, but I had already turned away, wondering if anyone would try to stop us from entering the neighborhood. There were no cops or firefighters in sight. It was worth a shot.

I started walking back toward the road block. There was no police cruiser, like on the first street, so maybe we could pass through unmolested.

Everyone else soon caught up to walk down the sidewalk with me. The smell of smoke was thick in the air. You'd think I'd be used to the scent by now, given how often I set things on fire, but I still found it unpleasant. It wasn't the nice scent of a roaring campfire, but the scent of an entire home burning down, filled with plastics, fabrics, and irreplaceable memories.

"What are we even looking for?" Sam asked from my right as Chase reached my left.

"The scent or sight of demons or werewolves," I explained, "and maybe the address of whatever home is on fire. If this is connected to the RV park fire, discovering whose home it is might be useful."

"We could just get that information from the

news," he muttered.

"And the demon scent?" I countered. "Do you think the news would report on that?"

He sighed. The neighborhood around us wasn't entirely quiet. People were in and out of their houses, loading valuables into their cars, just in case. It wasn't likely the fire would spread. There weren't a lot of trees around, and I was sure the firefighters were well into handling it, given the presence of the road blocks, but I didn't blame them for being worried. Better to store all your valuables up only to unpack them, than to risk the small chance of losing them.

I began to walk more easily as the smoke grew thicker. Since residents were still in the neighborhood, we probably wouldn't get in trouble for walking around. We could just pretend we'd left our house to come and gawk. Just a couple of pesky kids, officers, nothing to see here.

Lucy moved around Sam to step ahead of the group. She'd worn lighter colors today against the heat, and fit right into the suburban neighborhood. No one would ever guess she could crush their windpipe in the blink of an eye. Everyone else appeared normal too, in tee shirts and sneakers, or sandals in Allison's case. I, however, probably looked a little out of place in my all black outfit and black boots, but I was beyond caring. Anyone who had a problem with the way I looked could have a private meeting with one of my boots.

Lucy sniffed the air as we continued down the neighborhood street, then slowed down for us to catch up with her. "Nothing out of the ordinary yet," she whispered, then continued walking.

The burning home came into view. Flames still licked at the roof, darting out of shattered windows, while the firefighters focused heavy streams of water on it.

We continued toward the building as close as we dared. There were plenty of other neighborhood gawkers about, so no one paid us any attention. I tried to pick the homeowners out of the crowd, but no one seemed to be crying about the burning building.

I glanced to my side at Lucy.

She crossed her arms, worry creasing her brow. "It's difficult to pick up scents with all the smoke. I might have to walk around a bit. If I land right on top of a supernatural scent trail, it should be strong enough to distinguish."

I glanced at the gathered crowd, then turned around to address our group. "Shall we mingle? See if we can figure out who owns the house?"

Everyone nodded, then Chase added. "Let's form two groups, just in case."

I reached out an inviting hand toward him. "Partner?"

He took my hand in his. "You got it."

I ignored the collective sigh from Lucy, Allison, and Sam, then pulled Chase into the crowd. I scanned the gawkers, all pushed back behind police tape to keep them out of the way, wondering who'd be most likely to give me information. I spotted a few teenagers, hanging out with their skateboards in hand while pointing at the flames with their free appendages.

"Hey," I said as I approached them, acting natural. "Does anyone know what started the fire?"

The nearest guy didn't seem to think much of our approach. He ran his hand through his shaggy hair and answered, "Nah, at least not that I've heard. I did hear one of the cops mentioning something about some sort of accelerant. They're having trouble putting it out."

I lifted a fingernail up to my teeth in thought. Maybe the people evacuating their homes weren't doing so prematurely. "Who lives, I mean *lived* there?"

The boy glanced at me again, this time with a measure of suspicion in his blue eyes. Still, he answered, "Some guy. Keeps to himself mostly. Pretty sure he lived alone."

I glanced at the burning house, then back to the boy. "A place that big just for a single guy?"

He shrugged, then turned his back to dismiss me in favor of talking to his friends.

"The plot thickens," I muttered.

Chase frowned as we took a few steps away from the crowd. "Are we more interested in the possible accelerant, or in the oddity of a single guy living alone in a big home in a family neighborhood?"

"Both," I said, deep in thought. "It would be nice to know if an accelerant was used at the RV park too, but the person we would normally go to for that information is missing."

Chase looked back at the fire. "It has to all be connected, doesn't it?" he whispered. "First with what happened to Art, then the RV park, and now Abel and the other missing wolves?"

I nodded. "I don't understand this random fire though, if it is even connected at all."

His gray eyes met mine, his brow creased with worry. "It could go in line with the theory of you being set up. A fire demon comes to town, and residences begin to burn? If the person who lived in this house was something supernatural . . . " he trailed off.

I watched the flames. Under the deluge of water, they were finally beginning to die down. An extensive amount of damage had been done to the house, enough where I guessed the remains would simply be bulldozed before something else could be built. There would be little left to salvage. Had it been burned just to frame me? I wasn't sure. Usually when someone in the supernatural community wanted you out of the way, they killed you. I couldn't fathom why someone would go to all of the trouble just to set me up. If it was connected to the missing wolves, our mysterious enemy was either extremely powerful, or we were dealing with a group.

My phone buzzed in my pocket. I turned my back on the smoldering remains of the house, then pulled it out to answer it.

"We're ready to go when you are," Devin said as soon as I held the phone to my ear.

"Good," I breathed.

He was silent for a moment. "What, no giving me a hard time about not starting our call with inane niceties?"

I snorted. "By inane niceties, you mean saying *hello*? I'm more concerned with the second arson of our trip."

"I thought I told you to go hide out," he chided.

I put my free hand on my hip, though he couldn't see it. "We were on our way," I growled, "but we saw the fire and decided to stop." I glanced around to make sure no one was near enough to listen in on me, besides Chase, of course. "A spectator claimed the police thought some sort of accelerant was used."

"Find somewhere to stay, then come get us," he instructed. "And don't stop at any more burning buildings. We'll discuss all of the possibilities in person."

I pursed my lips in irritation, wanting to talk about the possibilities right then, but I decided not to argue. I'd spotted Lucy, Allison, and Sam approaching through the slowly dispersing crowd. I'd discuss things with them instead.

"Where are you?" I sighed into the phone.

"Jason's apartment."

I nodded, though he couldn't see it. "See you soon." I hung up before he could hang up first. These werewolves were really killing my already poor phone etiquette.

I returned my phone to my pocket, then looked to Lucy.

She shook her head. "I caught a few whiffs of werewolf in the crowd, but that doesn't really mean anything. Anything closer to the house just smelled like smoke, though maybe we can pick something up after the police clear out."

I sighed and started walking. Everyone fell into step around me. "We need to find a place to stay." I glanced around us once more, but no one was near. "Then I'll go pick up Devin and Jason."

"Another hotel?" Allison asked quietly.

I nodded. "A little further away from the latest arson this time. Once we're all together, I'll contact Eric."

Everyone remained silent. My stomach growled, reminding me that we'd skipped breakfast. Yes, food and a good regrouping were in order. Both important steps in any ongoing investigation. Xoe's Detective Agency, open for business.

# Chapter 10

Roughly forty minutes later, we arrived at our new hotel room with bags of fast food in hand. I glanced at the beds with matching green comforters, feeling a pang of sadness that I'd spend another night without Alexius at the foot of my bed. Hopefully he was having fun with Dorrie.

"I should go retrieve Devin and Jason," I announced once everyone was safe inside the room. At least, as safe as they were going to be with a murderer/arsonist/possible-portal-maker on the loose.

"You don't want to eat first?" Chase asked.

I glanced at the fast food bags piled on the table and found I had little appetite. "I'd rather get everyone together first. It worries me leaving you guys alone after all that has happened."

He put a comforting arm around me. "It should only take a few minutes, right?"

"I can come and grab one of them," Sam offered, moving to stand beside us.

I shook my head. "Strength in numbers. I don't want just three people alone, even for a few minutes." So maybe I was being paranoid, but my paranoia had kept me alive on more than one occasion. I wasn't about to give up the habit now.

I pulled away from Chase and gave him a quick peck on the cheek. "I'll be right back."

I closed my eyes and envisioned Jason's apartment. It was that simple. Since I'd been there before, having experienced all the nuances of the place, traveling there was easy. A few moments later, I appeared in a red cloud of smoke. I swatted my hand in front of my face, clearing it away. Jason and Devin stood before me in the middle of the small living room.

"It's about time," Devin sniped, straightening the lapels on his expensive black suit.

I rolled my eyes. "Sorry for keeping you waiting, your majesty." I softened my expression into a smile as I turned to Jason.

He wore his usual jeans, but the flannel was missing, replaced by a white teeshirt. It was a smart move since our destination was the desert.

"I'd take a moment to exchange inane pleasantries," I smirked at Devin, "but I don't like leaving everyone else vulnerable in Nevada, so who's first?"

Devin stepped forward. "I'll go."

Jason rocked back and forth on his feet with his hands in his pockets. "I suppose I'll see you when you get back," he said to me with a kindly gaze.

I nodded, then held out my hand for Devin. He took it and I envisioned our hotel room. A moment later, we were enveloped in the scent of fast food, filling the room with my odorless red smoke.

Sam looked up from his perch on the bed, his

mouth full of fries. "I wish my traveling looked like that," he said around his food, his eyes focused on the smoke as it dissipated.

I sighed, let go of Devin's hand, then disappeared again.

Reappearing in front of Jason, I held out my hand. "Ready?" I asked.

He stepped forward and took my hand. "As I'll ever be."

I closed my eyes, envisioning the hotel room.

"And Xoe?" he said.

I opened my eyes.

"It's good to see you," he finished.

I smiled at him faintly, then closed my eyes. Moments later we were back in the hotel room, which suddenly seemed crowded with seven people.

Chase eyed mine and Jason's grasped hands, which I promptly dropped. There was no reason for awkwardness. I *had* to hold his hand. Not that I was going to remind Chase of that out loud.

Seeming to recover, Chase reached into the fast food bag resting beside him on the bed, then held out a burger to me.

I took it and sat beside him, then looked up at Jason and Devin. "We bought extra food in case either of you are hungry."

"Umm . . . " Sam cut in nervously, glancing conspiratorially at Lucy.

I narrowed my eyes at him. "Let me guess, the extra food is already gone?"

"Well we *did* skip breakfast," Sam replied, as if

he'd been terribly put out.

"We already ate," Jason explained, letting Sam off the hook. He took a seat on my other side, running his fingers absentmindedly through his scruffy brown hair. At least to others it would seem an absentminded gesture. I knew it was the equivalent of his nervous tick.

Devin retrieved a chair from the room's small desk, since the beds now each had three people on them. He flicked his eyes to Sam as he sat. "I'm glad to see you've decided to make yourself useful."

I raised an eyebrow at Devin, waiting for an explanation.

"I tried to call him about Emma's father, as you suggested," he explained. "He claimed he was far too busy to hunt down a human man."

I gave Sam a *you should have helped them* look.

He didn't so much as flinch. "Don't look at me like that. I had an armful of library books when he called, and had just spent my hard earned money on alchemy supplies for Dorrie. What more do you want from me?"

I smirked. "You bought Dorrie alchemy supplies?"

He grunted. "It was either that or play another tedious game of Checkers." He moved his gaze to Chase. "I don't know *how* you live with her."

Chase simply smiled, though I knew he would rather not be living with Dorrie. Or really, he'd just rather not be living in my dad's house, which was now *my* house. I was more than happy to have him

120

living there, but he felt he should get his own place. Fortunately he'd had no time to look for one, what with my constant need for attention. Or at least my constant *in danger* status.

"Can we *please* get to business?" Devin asked tiredly.

I frowned at him. "What has you so cranky?"

He slouched back against his chair. "Abel is missing, so not only have I been *your* pack leader, I've also been fielding all of his phone calls. It has been an exhausting morning."

That brought to mind one of our earlier theories. "So you're like, the de facto coalition leader?"

He shook his head, smoothing a hand over his well-groomed blond hair. "Hardly. A new leader would need to be voted on. It is simply well known that I work closely with Abel, and that I'm the best way to get a hold of him."

"So, who would be lobbying for the position of coalition leader if a vote were called for?" I pressed.

He paused and narrowed his eyes suspiciously. "Why do you want to know? You're not hoping to run for the position, are you?"

I snorted. "No thanks. We were just earlier hypothesizing possible reasons for someone to kidnap Abel. If there were say, a suspicious wolf who'd love to slip into the position, maybe we could question him or her."

The corner of his lip ticked up into a partial smile. "A *suspicious* wolf?"

I shrugged. "You know, maybe he'd be wearing

a black cape, probably has a goatee, carries a sword disguised as a cane . . . "

His half-smile turned into a full smirk. "I'll look into it, but while we're here, perhaps we should focus o n *all* of the missing wolves. Find one and perhaps we'll find them all, including Abel."

"And that leads us to Eric and Iva," I explained. "I think we need to question both of them more thoroughly. If this is all a set up, I have to wonder if they truly have missing wolves, or if it was all a ruse to draw me in."

Devin stood. "Good. Let us start with Iva."

I frowned, glancing down at my uneaten burger.

Seeing my hesitation, he sighed and sat, gesturing for me to eat. I unwrapped my burger and took a bite, displeased to find that it had gotten cold, and a little soggy. "Iva is going to be pissed to see you," I commented before taking another bite. I swallowed, forcing the second gulp down my throat. "I promised I wouldn't alert the coalition about the missing wolves until the end of the week."

He narrowed his eyes at me. "Unwise promises aside, I imagine she'll understand once she learns that Abel is missing as well."

"Unless she's responsible for his disappearance," Chase countered.

Devin seemed to think for a moment. "Seeing her reaction might be worthwhile," he mused. "If she shows little surprise, or an inordinate amount of surprise, we can surmise that she already knew he was missing."

"True," I said around another bite of my burger. "We'll all go down to her house and judge together."

Devin glanced around at everyone in the room. "All of us?"

I nodded. "I also have a theory that the kidnapper can form portals. I'm not leaving anyone alone to get sucked up into who knows what realm."

His eyes widened. "I thought you were the only one who could do that."

"We all thought that," I explained, "and it may be the case, but if the destroyed room at our last hotel was only a mock-portal, whoever faked it did a very good job, especially considering few have experienced the damage created by my portals."

"Nix probably has a good idea of how it looks," Chase chimed in speculatively.

I took another bite of my cold burger and thought about that possibility. On one hand, it would make sense for her to be connected to this mystery, on the other, what could her possible end goal be? From what we'd gathered, she'd intended me harm simply because she'd been working with my grandmother, but my grandmother was dead, and we'd gotten rid of her ghost. Nix didn't strike me as the type who'd try to avenge the death of a woman she didn't particularly seem to like, but who knew?

I took one more bite of my burger, then discarded it. The cold lump wasn't sitting well in my tummy, and I didn't want to barf all over Iva when we saw her. Unless it would make her tell the truth, then I'd barf away. Interrogation by vomit, the next step after violence fails.

I rose and turned my gaze to Sam. "Keep your ghosts on the lookout for Nix. See if you can figure out if she's here, or still in the dream realm. Right now our best leads are Iva and Eric, so that's where we'll start."

"We won't all fit in the car," Lucy pointed out, always the voice of reason.

I frowned, she was right. After a moment's thought, I amended, "You guys take the car and Chase and I will meet you there. If we run into trouble before you arrive, I'll just poof us back out."

"You don't think she'll run if we all just show up there?" Jason asked.

I shrugged. "You have a point. Maybe Chase and I will go in first. A visit from just the two of us wouldn't seem out of the ordinary, since we were the only ones to attend the initial meeting."

Devin nodded. "We'll park out of sight and fan out around the house, just in case she tries to run. There's always the possibility that she really is just looking for her missing wolves, and therefore may be a valuable ally."

I bit my lip, not liking the idea of anyone *fanning out*. We were stronger if we stuck together. I could easily transport Chase and I away from danger, but if it came to it, Sam wouldn't be able to save everyone.

Jason watched my face as if he knew just what I was thinking. "We'll be careful," he assured.

I frowned. "Sometimes careful isn't good

enough."

"Well it's the best we can do," Devin interrupted.

I took a steadying breath. He was right. I nodded. "Call me when you guys are a few minutes away and we'll meet you there."

Everyone nodded their assent. Sam patted Chase's shoulder as he walked past, then looked at me. "Stop worrying, boss. If anyone tries to ambush us, my ghosts will see them from a mile away."

I lifted an eyebrow at him. "Boss?"

He smirked. "Seems a fitting title."

I shook my head, fighting a small smile as everyone made their way to the door. "We'll see you all soon," I called after them.

The door shut, and suddenly Chase and I were alone in the room.

"I *really* don't like this," he said softly, his gaze on the closed door. He turned to me. "I'd almost feel better if it was just the two of us going. We'd be able to escape quickly and not risk losing anyone."

I pursed my lips in thought, then shook my head. "They never would agree to it. None of them are the *run and hide* types."

"Sam is."

I turned my eyes up to him. "Yet he's here, *helping*."

His shoulders slumped. "I still don't trust him. I can't help it."

I took his hand. "He's sneaky, but he cares about you. I can tell."

"I guess I'm just not used to having people care about me." He cringed, then met my eyes. "Sorry, that sounded much less melodramatic in my head."

I gave his hand a squeeze, then drew him to sit on the bed beside me. We still had a few minutes before we should leave, since it would take the others a while to reach Iva's.

"My entire life, I thought I'd hate my dad if I ever met him," I explained. "I thought there was no excuse for abandoning me and my mom."

"You know why he did it," he began.

I held up a hand to stop him. "I know, and that's exactly what I'm getting at. My dad made the wrong choice, even though he had noble intentions. Even though I *did* get to live sixteen years of a nice normal life because of him, I still sometimes feel angry about his choice. I feel angry that I'll never get back the time I could have had with him."

"He made a mistake," Chase said softly.

I nodded. "Yeah, and Sam has made mistakes. You know how I feel about *some* of his mistakes, but we can't hold them against him forever."

He smiled, then kissed me on the cheek, seeing what I was trying to do. "And when did you become so forgiving? You're usually the first to jump on the vengeance train."

I shrugged. "I guess I've reached the point where I've made so many mistakes, I can no longer fault anyone else for theirs. I can't say what I would have done if I'd been in my dad's shoes, and you can't say what you would have done if you'd been in

Sam's. Everyone has their reasons for doing things, and he's here *now*." I held my hand back up before he could speak. "I know you want to believe that he's just trying to make things up to me, but I can see what he's trying to do. He wants a relationship with his brother, and I don't blame him. He's far more alone in this world than either of us."

Chase wrapped his arm around me and pulled me close. "You really need to stop making so much sense. It's scary."

I pushed him away playfully. "I'm quite offended that everyone is so surprised by my occasional insights and displays of personal growth."

He pulled me back toward him and kissed me.

I lifted my hand and ran my fingers through his hair, thinking how much I'd like to leave everything behind to hang out with him, cozy in the underground, watching a fun movie. With me, Chase, Alexius, and Dorrie down there, it was almost like living with a family. Even Sam popping in wasn't half bad. Since we'd been on the road, I'd found that I'd missed my dad's house. It felt like home. As hard as my mom had tried to bridge the gap between us, things couldn't be like they were when I was growing up. I needed to form my own, new little life where I could feel comfortable with who and *what* I was.

I pulled away from the gentle kiss. "When all of this is over, I want you to consider not moving," I blurted.

He raised his eyebrows in surprise, his gray eyes wide.

"I want you to stay right where you are, and I want to live there with you. I want to find new adventures that have nothing to do with either of our pasts."

He grinned, and I exhaled in relief.

"So what do you think?" I pressed.

He pulled me close and kissed my cheek. "I think that if my smart, beautiful, and sometimes scary girlfriend wants me to live with her permanently, I'd be a fool to say no."

I laughed. "I'm glad to see you have excellent self preservation instincts, but seriously, is that a yes? You won't leave?"

He chuckled. "Well it wasn't like I was going to go *far*, but it's a yes. I'll live with you *wherever* you like."

I acknowledged his statement with a curt nod, unable to help my grin. My phone chose that moment to buzz beside me on the bed. I lifted it to see Jason calling, and answered.

"According to Lucy, we're a few minutes out from Iva's," he explained.

"We'll leave now," I replied.

We both hung up and I turned my attention back to Chase. "Now let's go save all of these werewolves so we can get on with our lives."

He nodded, taking my hand as we rose to our feet.

"I love you," he said, just as I was starting to envision Iva's front yard.

I smiled with my eyes still closed. "I'm going to

hold you to that once you realize what a total terror I am to live with full time."

"I can handle terror," he laughed.

We dissipated, and moments later appeared in Iva's front yard. At first I didn't realize anything was amiss, until I looked at the front door, which rested at a slight angle, dangling from broken hinges. No one would likely notice it from the street, but someone had definitely broken in.

I glanced at Chase to register that he'd noticed the door too, then sighed. "I'm going to hold you to that terror comment."

He squeezed my hand. "Do we investigate, or wait for the others?"

"The others are already here," a voice said from behind us. I didn't recognize the speaker.

Something hit me in the back of the head. I tried to turn around to see who'd attacked me, but my vision slowly faded to gray, obscuring the figures standing over me.

# Chapter 11

I awoke to darkness. Not pitch darkness, the moon and stars were overhead, but it was some time late at night. How many hours had I lost? More importantly, who in the heck was carrying me? I was cradled in someone's arms.

As alarm bells rang in my head I lashed out, burning whoever held me. I dropped to the ground and landed on my tailbone. The impact stole my breath and my head spun. I lifted a hand to my scalp to find it sticky with congealed blood.

"It's me," a pained voice said from above me.

"Jason?" I questioned. "Where are we?"

"In the middle of the desert," he explained. "I was just trying to keep us hidden until you woke up."

I tried to stand, but still felt too dizzy. Sand scratched my palms as I leaned heavily on my arms to keep myself from sprawling across the ground. "Where is everyone else?"

"Taken," he explained, moving to kneel beside me so I could see his face in the moonlight. "We had parked a few houses down, then spread out to encircle the perimeter of the property. I came around from the front and saw two men just as they snuck up and attacked you. I rushed forward, but there were more of them. Devin and Lucy joined the fray, but it was clear we would lose. Chase demanded I take you and run. It was a logical choice. I'm faster than everyone else."

I held a hand up to stop him. "Slow down. So we just left them all behind?"

He nodded. "The attackers chose to incapacitate you first, likely either afraid you would travel away from them, or set them on fire. Or else they simply wanted to take everyone else and leave you there."

"You keep saying *take*. How did they *take* them."

"They created a portal," he explained. "Right in broad daylight, in a human neighborhood. I barely managed to escape it."

A myriad of emotions hit me, bringing on hot tears to run down my face. My head began to throb even harder as the chilly night air stung my wound.

Jason placed a hand on my shoulder. "Xoe, we'll find them."

I shook my head and was overcome with another wave of dizziness. If I was feeling this bad, the blow to my head likely would have killed a human. "How?" I cried. "They took *everyone*. We have no way of finding them."

"We have two choices," he explained calmly. "We can either go to the demon underground and search for information, or we can go back to Shelby and enlist the witches to help us."

"So the people who attacked us were demons?" I asked, trying to piece everything together.

"Some demons, some vampires," he explained.

I took a deep, shaky breath. This was no time for hysterics. We needed to get to work. "What did the vampires look like? Did you recognize any of them?"

He shook his head.

"Was one in his mid-twenties, of Asian decent, short but messy hair?"

He shook his head again. "Not that I saw."

I patted down my pockets then let out a sigh of relief when I realized I still had my phone. I retrieved it and lit up the screen, then groaned. "Where in the heck are we? I don't have any service."

"We're in the middle of the desert," he explained. "I didn't want to risk anyone finding us before you'd regained consciousness."

I reached out and grabbed his hand. I might not have been capable of standing, but I was pretty sure I could still transport us. "I need to make a call. Depending on whether or not that person answers, we'll then go to Shelby and find Cynthia."

Jason nodded. I closed my eyes and envisioned the first place that came to mind, the burned down RV park. I didn't want to go anywhere our enemies might look for us, and who in their right mind would go back to the scene of an arson after all of their friends had been kidnapped by way of portal?

We appeared crouched in the darkness, encircled by the skeletal remains of the burned RVs. I glanced around for signs of life, but we seemed to be alone. The place stunk of smoke and ash.

Jason stood and offered me a hand up, which I took gratefully. I wasn't sure I was quite ready to stand, but I'd risk it. I was going to have to do a lot more than stand before the night was through.

I skimmed through my contacts until I found Eric's number and pushed send.

He answered on the second ring. "Would you believe that you're just the person I was desperately hoping to talk to?" he asked.

"I take it that means Iva is missing?"

He was silent for several seconds. "Did you go to her house?"

"Yes," I replied, "but I didn't get a chance to go inside before we were attacked by demons and a few vampires."

"Demons?" he questioned, though he didn't seem overly surprised. "Where are you now?"

"I'm not telling you anything until I'm sure you're not part of this."

He was silent again. "Just tell me what you want me to do and I'll do it."

"For Iva?" I questioned, wondering if my suspicions about them having a relationship were correct.

"Yes."

"Tell me where you are."

He sighed. "I just arrived at Iva's. I was going to look things over, see if I missed any clues as to who has taken her."

I hung up, then looked to Jason. "I'll be right back," I assured.

Before he could argue I envisioned Iva's house and dissipated. I caught Eric just as he was reaching for the slightly ajar front door. I took a moment to be astounded that no police cars were present after a portal had been made in the front yard, then I grabbed him before he had time to turn around. I thought of the RV park again, and back we went.

Jason crossed his arms and glared at me as we appeared before him. "I do not appreciate you running off whilst injured," he chided.

I released Eric so he could stumble away from me. *Traveling* could be a little jarring for first timers.

I shrugged at Jason apologetically. "I didn't want to give him any time to set a trap." I nodded in Eric's direction.

Eric straightened, seeming to regain his composure. "Why would *I* set a trap?"

"Why wouldn't you?" I countered petulantly.

I couldn't see that clearly in the darkness, but he seemed to be clenching and unclenching his fists in irritation. He wore a similar black outfit to the previous night, but it was wrinkled and his shirt was untucked. Maybe it was the *same* outfit, and he really had been running around all that time trying to find his girlfriend.

"Look," I said. "I don't know who's side you're on, but if Iva was taken by the same people who took my friends, I'll get her back. You just need to tell me *everything* you know about what's going on."

The moonlight reflected in his eyes as he glared at me. It was looking like my track record with vampires wasn't going to improve, then his shoulders slumped, and his glare faded.

"It's all a set up," he breathed. "All of it."

My jaw dropped. While I'd been suspecting just that, I hadn't expected him to so blatantly admit it.

"Your demon kin wanted you *dethroned*, as it were," he continued. "Art hired me, but there are many others. They're not happy that you get to live in the demon city with a certain measure of respect, while they're left with nothing. If you died, your home and status would go to your next of kin, however distant. They want to take over your life."

I shook my head and let out a shaky breath. My distant relatives wanted to steal my life, just like my grandmother, though she'd wanted to take over my body too. I wasn't sure what was so great about the things I'd been afforded, but then again, I had no idea how bad life might have been for them.

"So where do you come in?" I asked.

"As I said, Art hired me," he explained. "He didn't want to risk being linked to your downfall by setting everything up himself. I'd heard of your involvement in solving other cases for the werewolf commission, so I set up a plan to lure you in. I helped the demons working with Art kidnap a few wolves. They guaranteed they would not harm them. I had been trying for the past week to convince Iva to contact you, but she's stubborn, and wanted to find the missing wolves herself. Then lo and behold, you show up in town, doing that part of my job for me."

"So Iva didn't know it was all a trick?" I interrupted.

He shook his head. "She thought her people

were actually missing. I didn't want her involved in the scheme any more than necessary."

I glanced around us uneasily. We'd been out in the open for a while. "What are the demons planning?" I demanded.

"They're setting you up," he explained. "They want to bring you to the attention of the demon council. The arsons, the missing wolves, including the coalition leader, they want to blame it all on you. You're being framed."

"But why?" I asked breathlessly. "What did I ever do to them?"

"Your father inherited your grandmother's power and high standing within the demon community, and now it's all been passed on to you. The rest of your kin were left weak and destitute."

"So they enacted this whole elaborate scheme because they're jealous?" I asked, exasperated.

He sighed. "If you're found guilty before the demon council, you'll be killed, and all of your inheritance and demon status will go to your kin. If they simply kill you, the council will punish *them*."

I shook my head in utter disbelief. "And why are you telling us all of this now?"

He clenched his fists again. "I want Iva back. Her being taken was not part of the deal. I fear there is a more nefarious slant to their plan than they led me to believe. I don't know what they intend to do with that many werewolves, but it cannot be good. I've given up hope that Iva's people will be returned as promised, let alone Iva herself."

I glanced at Jason to see what he thought, but his face was unreadable. I'd heard about the demon council before. My father had been worried about me being brought to their attention, both after we killed Bartimus, and when I'd accidentally brought Dorrie back from the dream realm. While the werewolves were more keen on policing the human world, if a demon caused enough mayhem, the council would step in. I'd inadvertently caused quite a bit of mayhem over the past year, and wouldn't be surprised if I was already on their radar.

I wrapped my arms tightly around myself, feeling vulnerable. I needed to focus on what was important. I could figure out the rest later. I narrowed an eye at Eric. "Where are they keeping the wolves?"

He shook his head. "I don't know. I imagine in the underground. It would be difficult otherwise to keep that many werewolves contained."

"Unless they simply killed them all," Jason added.

I glared at him. He wasn't helping.

I turned back to Eric. "What about the other vampires working with the demons?"

He shook his head. "They probably hired them, just like they did with me."

My jaw tensed, I turned away from Eric to take Jason's hand. "I have a plan," I whispered.

Eric held up his hands before we could *poof* away. "What about me? You're just going to leave me here?"

I eyed him cooly. "Yes, and if all of my friends

come out of this unharmed, I might even let you live, though I wouldn't want to be *you* once Abel and the other wolves are back."

"I'm a vampire," he growled. "I'm not afraid of demons and werewolves."

I smirked. "You should be."

We disappeared in a wash of smoke, only to reappear moments later in Jason's dark apartment back in Shelby. Neither of us moved to turn on the lights. There was enough moonlight streaming through the windows to see well enough.

Jason stepped away from me, then pulled his cell phone out of his pocket. "Do we call Cynthia?"

I raised my eyebrows at him in surprise.

He waited, then asked, "Do we not?"

I smiled. "We do, I just didn't expect you to immediately guess my plan."

He smiled back. "Summon Chase and Sam, then have them lead us to where the wolves and Allison are being kept? It's simple enough to possibly work."

I nodded. "Yeah, unless the kidnappers have enlisted witches too."

"It's worth a shot, at least." He pressed a few buttons then lifted the phone to his ear.

I bit my lip, waiting impatiently. If Cynthia couldn't summon Chase or Sam, I didn't know what we were going to do. I'd always had people to fall back on. My dad, Abel, Devin, the list went on. Now it was just me and Jason. Not that Jason wasn't a fine resource in his own right, he was a bounty hunter by trade, and knew his way around the paranormal community, but he was still just a single vampire. He didn't have Abel and Devin's resources, nor my dad's knowledge and power. It scared me that we didn't have any backup. Besides my mom, everyone I loved the most had been taken. They were all I had left. I couldn't lose them now.

After what seemed like an eternity of waiting, Cynthia picked up, judging by Jason's change in stance. He asked if she would meet us. She apparently said no, because next he resorted to telling her she could meet us, or we'd come find her. A moment later, he hung up the phone.

"She'll be here in twenty minutes," he explained, lowering his phone into his pocket.

I nodded. "Do you think it was the best idea to threaten her? We are asking for her help, after all."

"She wouldn't have come otherwise."

I let out a long breath. "You're probably right. I just don't know what we're going to do if she won't help us."

He put a hand on my shoulder, drawing my attention to his face. "She'll help," he assured. "As much as she likes to act tough, she knows she's only alive because of you, and she likes having the option of that protection. She's not going to alienate the only powerful member of the supernatural community she has ties to."

Feeling suddenly overcome with exhaustion, I moved away from him and slumped down onto the small couch. "You're right. Cynthia is practical above all else."

He turned on a lamp, adding a small measure of light to the otherwise dark room, then sat down beside me. He reached out to gingerly touch the side of my head.

I cringed, only then remembering the head wound. It was well on its way to healing, but I still had congealed blood in my hair. "Maybe I should clean up."

He nodded and let his hand drop. "Unless you think the sight of your bloody head will inspire sympathy in Cynthia."

I snorted. "She has no sympathy for the devil. She'd rather demons not exist at all."

He smiled wistfully. "You're probably right. You know where the clean towels are, so help yourself."

I stood, feeling a small pang of discomfort. I knew where the clean towels were because I'd spent plenty of time in Jason's apartment. He didn't seem to feel awkward about it. I did.

I left him sitting on the couch as I made my way toward the bathroom, stopping at the hall closet to retrieve a dark blue towel that hopefully wouldn't be ruined by a few bloodstains.

I flipped on the bathroom light and sealed myself inside. I set the towel on the edge of the small porcelain sink, then leaned against it, bracing myself with my arms. I took a shaky breath, then peered at my self in the mirror. I looked pale and tired. Blood had dried on one side of my face and hair, clumping my blonde locks together and turning them a muted red. I was glad I'd chosen to wear all black, or my clothes would have shown everything. I'd been in such a rush after waking that I hadn't even thought to retrieve our luggage from the hotel room in Nevada, but the clothes felt inconsequential, not when I felt like I was going to lose almost everyone who was important to me.

Wanting to be clean and ready by the time Cynthia arrived, I turned on the water in the sink and started scrubbing. Red rivulets ran down my face to drip into the sink, coloring the quickly draining water a light pink. As I scrubbed, tears hit me. The moment alone in the bathroom had been a bad idea. I needed to be planning. I couldn't think about the implications of the day's events. I simply needed to remedy them.

As I continued to scrub, I went over everything Eric had said. My distant demon relatives were trying to set me up so the demon council would kill me. Not only had they taken away my loved ones, they wanted my life and everything my father had left me. They could go to hell.

I finished scrubbing and dried myself off with the towel. My head still ached, but there was no sign of fresh blood. Now if only I didn't look like an exhausted, nearly drowned sewer rat, we'd be good.

I threw the towel on a wall hook, then left the bathroom, only to be hit by the smell of coffee. I instantly relaxed.

Jason walked out of the small kitchenette and handed me a plate with two sandwiches stacked on top of each other. "You've barely eaten today," he explained, "and you'll need your strength. As I recall, summoning demons fully requires a great deal of *your* energy, as well as Cynthia's."

I nodded and took the sandwiches gratefully, then glanced past him at the coffee pot.

He smiled. "Almost ready."

We both moved back to the couch.

"I've been thinking," I began, "that we should probably summon Chase first. If Sam were in any condition to travel, he would use his ghosts. I'm worried that he's unconscious or . . . " I trailed off, not wanting to think that *everyone* could already be dead.

"Unless they're all somehow contained against traveling or being summoned," Jason added thoughtfully. "Didn't your grandmother manage such an environment before?"

I nodded. "With the help of witches. It was how she kept my dad trapped before she killed him."

"Our adversaries have planned things out well thus far. I wouldn't be surprised if they've taken precautions against summoning."

I shrugged. "We still should try. It would be stupid if we could have summoned them out, but simply dismissed it as an option."

"Agreed, although I'm wondering if we should contact Lela and your remaining pack members to donate their energy to the summoning. I don't want you getting worn out for no reason. You already look like you're about to keel over."

I snorted. "Well aren't you quite the flatterer?"

He gave my shoulder a gentle pat. "You know

what I mean. Now eat your sandwiches."

I looked down at the plate in my lap, not really feeling hungry, but he was right. I needed my strength for whatever lay before us. I picked one up, but before taking a bite, conceded, "Maybe *just* call Lela. I know she'll be glad to help, but not the others. I don't want to ask near strangers to lend me their energy."

"Emma and Siobhan aren't strangers," he countered.

I shook my head. "Close enough, and they have their own problems to deal with right now."

Jason seemed deep in thought as I began to eat the first sandwich. Peanut butter and jelly, mmm. After a few minutes he turned his gaze back to me.

I raised an eyebrow in question, my mouth full of sandwich.

"I was just thinking about Emma's father," he explained, "and how he's somehow managed to evade us all. I can't help but wonder . . . " he trailed off.

I swallowed another bite of sandwich. "Yes?"

"Well I wonder if his appearance is somehow connected to all of this. Just one more distraction. Maybe the kidnappers are helping him stay hidden. If they have the capability to travel back and forth from the underground, they could be hiding him there."

"It's a thought," I agreed, "but not one that really helps us since we probably stand as much chance of finding him as we do everyone else."

Jason nodded and stood. "I suppose you're right. I'll call Lela and ask her to come over."

I moved on to the second sandwich, hoping

Cynthia would arrive soon. If we couldn't summon anyone, we'd just have to take to the underground and hope we could find some clues. Maybe Dorrie would know how to help. She had to remain hidden in my dad's house, but she often surprised me with her information on the demon world. Driving cabs for demonic dream travelers for hundreds of years had made her a veritable wellspring of odd knowledge. If nothing else, maybe she could provide us with some helpful alchemical potions.

We had a plan A and a plan B. It was a good start. Unfortunately we'd likely need plans C, D, and E if any of us hoped to come out of this alive, and I was fresh out of ideas.

## Chapter 12

I sat on the couch drinking coffee next to Lela, who'd arrived before Cynthia even though we'd called her twenty minutes later. Cynthia was late. Very, *very* late. My nerves were twanging with anxiety.

Lela sat perfectly still beside me. Her long, black hair was woven into a simple braid that fell over the shoulder of her lightweight, tan leather jacket. Beneath the jacket she wore a white cotton tee shirt and jeans. She'd shown up ready to fight, summon demons, or whatever else I asked of her. Really she was probably the only pack member that truly listened to my orders, and I'd never been as appreciative of it as I was in that moment.

Jason left the kitchen and returned to us with a mug of green tea in hand, which he offered to Lela. She took it gratefully, but didn't speak.

"Maybe we should call Cynthia again," I suggested. "She should have been here by now."

He nodded, pulled out his phone, and selected her number. After a minute, he lowered the phone. "Straight to voicemail."

"Crap," I muttered. "This is not good."

"I say we wait here for ten more minutes, then we go underground," Jason stated.

I looked up at him. "You think she was taken like everyone else?"

He nodded. "I wouldn't be surprised."

I sighed. "Neither would I, but I just don't understand how they're able to act so quickly. They knew what hotel and which room Jessica, Chris, and Matt were staying in. They knew to intercept Abel on his way to Nevada. Then they knew how to find us outside of Iva's house."

Jason looked down at the cellphone in his hand, his eyes wide. "Our phones," he muttered, then looked back up to me. "They're somehow tapping into our phone calls."

"W-what?" I stammered in disbelief.

"I was with Devin when he talked to Abel before he left for Nevada," he explained. "Abel told him what route he'd be taking. Then I called you when we were halfway to Iva's house, letting anyone listening know where we'd be. Did you ever say over the phone which hotel you'd be staying at the night Abel's three wolves were taken?"

My breath hitched in realization. "I told Abel where we were staying."

"But you called me to come over here," Lela interrupted. "and no one attacked me on the way."

"Yeah but you don't have the power to summon demons," I countered. "Cynthia would have been the priority." I turned back to Jason. "So no more cellphones. We'll wait ten more minutes for Cynthia, then we'll go underground. If she shows up afterward, I'm sure she'll call."

Jason nodded, his expression somber, then looked down at his cell phone like it had betrayed him.

I took another sip of my coffee as we waited.

And waited.

Ten minutes went by, and Cynthia never showed.

I stood. "I'll have to take you guys down one at a time," I explained, though Jason already knew, "but I'm afraid to leave either of you alone."

"Take Lela first," Jason instructed. "I'll be fine."

I nodded, not believing his words, but I took Lela's hand, planning an ultra-fast turnaround.

One moment we were in Jason's apartment, and the next my dad's kitchen. I left Lela without any explanation, then went back for Jason, breathing a sigh of relief to see that he was right where I'd left him.

He took my hand wordlessly, and I thought of my dad's house again. When we arrived, Dorrie was in the kitchen, glaring at Lela with threatening eyes. Lela had backed herself into a corner, as far away from Dorrie as possible.

Dorrie's sparkling eyes lit when she saw me, though she quickly turned her gaze back to Lela. "Do you know this woman, Pop Tart?"

I looked Dorrie up and down from her jean overalls, to her sparkly white skin, to her near-translucent white hair. She didn't seem terribly intimidating, but then again, I *knew* her. Of course I also knew that she was unbelievably strong. She'd accidentally broken my grandmother's neck with a simple tackle.

"She's with us," I explained. "We've got big problems."

A happy bark preceded Alexius as he came bounding into the kitchen. He jumped up as he reached me, bracing his front legs against my stomach. His claws scratched up my skin, but I didn't care. I knelt down in front of him to make him sit, then ruffled his fur.

Dorrie glanced past me at Jason, then returned her gaze to me. "Where's Chase?"

"Missing," I explained. "I think he's being held with many others somewhere in the underground. Some demons are trying to set me up in hopes the council will kill me."

Dorrie gasped.

Lela cautiously walked forward, glancing warily at Dorrie, lingering on her unusual hair and skin. "If they're down here," her eyes darted around as if she wondered where *here* was, "maybe I can sniff them out."

"There's a whole city out there," I gestured toward the front of the house, "and many other smaller areas and individual . . . lairs, for lack of a better word. We could be hunting around for weeks, and I don't think we have weeks."

"Especially if someone is trying to set you up to be investigated by the demon council," Dorrie added. "If they decide to come after you, there will be nowhere left to hide."

As if on cue, an ominous knock sounded on the front door in the next room over.

My eyes widened. I glanced around at my companions, settling on Dorrie. "Were you expecting company?" I whispered.

"Sam is the only other person who visits," she whispered back, "and he never knocks." She gestured for me to wait as she tip-toed into the next room.

I waited with my heartbeat thundering in my head, making it difficult to breathe.

A moment later she came scurrying back into the kitchen. "You have to get out of here!" she gasped, her voice a harsh whisper. "There are a bunch of official looking demons at the front door!"

"Where am I supposed to go?" I rasped back. "I can only travel with one person at a time."

Dorrie hurried toward me and took my hand. She gestured frantically for Lela and Jason to approach. They both did, then Dorrie crouched and put a hand on Alexius.

"Make a portal, Dumpling," she instructed. "Take us all to the dream world. It's the only place they won't be able to follow."

Lela and Jason both grabbed onto me too hard. I wasn't sure if I could travel with three people and a dog, but I couldn't leave anyone behind. I didn't have time to think about it. If the demon council really was at the door, we had to get out of there, *fast*.

I focused on creating a portal, knowing I would leave destruction in my wake. I felt a pang of guilt about destroying the kitchen my dad had repaired not long before he died, but I had no choice. I couldn't worry about it right then. Even if the council just wanted to question me, we didn't have the time, and we couldn't risk me being taken into custody.

I was overcome by the feeling of upward motion as the ceiling rushed forward to meet us. Before we hit, everything went black, then we were tossed onto hard pavement in various horizontal positions. I struggled to sit up, then looked around at the desolate bus station of the dream realm, the starting point for anyone traveling to other realms.

Lela staggered to her feet. "Where are we?" she gasped. She looked around frantically.

Fortunately, the shadowy shapes that stalked the depot were currently nowhere to be seen, else she might wet herself out of fear. She seemed close to doing so now.

Alexius glanced around curiously, remaining at my side.

Jason stood and helped me to my feet as Dorrie approached the benches of the depot. "We need to find a driver," she muttered. "I don't want to be here once those shadow monsters realize we've arrived."

I cringed, then glanced at Lela's panic stricken face. "I can *travel* between realms," I explained, "but I can only take one person at a time. I've never tried making portals to other areas of the dream world. They're more intended for traveling between different planes of reality."

Lela's eyes widened in horror. "I'm in a

152

different plane of reality?"

"Yes." I began to pace. "Maybe we should just go back to another area of the underground. We need to continue our search."

Dorrie approached my side and gripped my arm to stop my pacing. "They'll find you no matter where you go down there. It's too risky. What are you being framed for?"

"For kidnapping the werewolf coalition leader along with several other wolves, arson, oh, and maybe for my uncle's murder." I shrugged, feeling flustered. "Who knows? Maybe they've even somehow brought up how Bart died, or-" I stopped myself before mentioning Josie, since that had remained a secret few knew about.

"What's that?" Lela squeaked.

I followed her gaze to see a reflection in the window of the bus depot. It was huge, and seemed to writhe and change shape as it moved. Alexius started barking.

"Not something we want to stick around to see," I muttered. "Everybody grab onto me. I'm going to try to make a portal to another area of the dream world."

Within seconds everyone gripped my arms and shoulders, and Dorrie leaned down and curled her fingers around Alexius' collar with her free hand. I had only been to a few different areas within the dream world, and only one I could picture clearly. I closed my eyes and we all thrust upward. After a few dizzying seconds of movement, we landed hard in a puddle of goo. Gre-at. Just what we needed.

153

I struggled to stand in the sparkly black puddle, but it was incredibly slippery. Everyone else was stuck too. We all fumbled about, getting the goo all over our hands and clothing.

Jason made it out first, then offered me a gooey hand. I  grasped it hard to overcome the slipperiness, making traction difficult. I slowly made my way to the puddle's edge and onto dry land. Releasing Jason's hand, I took in our surroundings. The realm resembled something straight out of a Dracula movie. Scraggly black trees reached up toward an ominous dark sky, complete with an eerie full moon. A shiver ran up my spine, reminding me of my recent experience in this very realm. I'd died there, shortly before being brought back to life.

The others made it out of the puddle with audible sighs of relief. Then Alexius started whining.

"What is it?" I asked rhetorically.

He seemed to be watching something in the distance. His whine turned into a growl.

"I see smoke," Lela commented.

I followed her gaze. She was right. It was hard to see at first, but against the full moon, the smoke became illuminated. It was odd, but didn't necessarily mean anything. A few demons and other denizens lived in the dream world, brought there ages ago through portals. Travel to the dream realm used to be more frequent, back in the days when *drivers* like Dorrie were created, hundreds of years prior.

My mind jumped to the crazy old woman demon I'd encountered on my first trip to the dream realm. She'd tried to kill me, thinking I was my grandmother, and Dorrie had saved me. The smoke wasn't coming from the direction of her mansion though, and I wasn't even sure if she was still alive. Dorrie had thrown her through a wall, and we hadn't stuck around to see if it killed her.

I looked down at Alexius. He'd stopped barking, but was still staring in the direction of the smoke.

"Let's check it out," I sighed. "Alexius seems to think there's something interesting about this smoke."

"Well he *is* your spirit guide," Dorrie reminded me. "He's here to, you know, guide you."

"Hmph," I replied, thinking it more likely that Alexius was just curious.

Everyone fell into step around me as we made our way toward the smoke. I wracked my brain for possible ways to find the others. Ghosts would have been useful, but only Sam and Chase could control them. I couldn't see any way for me to see into the human or demon worlds while stuck in the dream realm.

Smaller puddles of ooze squelched beneath our shoes as we walked. They were more sparse in some areas of the realm, but where we were, they were nearly impossible to avoid.

We slowed down as we neared the smoke. There was a burned building not far off. It looked like it had once been a grand mansion, but now had smoldered down to rubble.

Alexius darted forward before I could stop him.

Feeling flustered and not wanting to call out his name to alert any possible inhabitants in the realm, I ran after him, but Jason and Lela soon outpaced me.

I watched as they ran toward the building. Dorrie probably could have outpaced me too, but remained by my side. I briefly considered *traveling* ahead, but we were almost there. Jason and Lela reached the ruined building, and stopped to look around. No one jumped out and attacked them.

Huffing and puffing, I arrived a moment later.

Alexius was sniffing all around the ruined building, carefully avoiding the piles of debris still smoking with heat. He paused near a ruined wall and let out a low growl.

I jogged to his side as the others searched about.

"What is it?" I asked, reaching the dog's side.

He continued to growl at the crumbling wall as a wispy shape formed. It seemed like it was made of vapor or smoke, but it pulled itself out of the wall and wafted toward me.

Alexius' fur bristled on his back as I stared at the small wisp. It was a ghost.

My first thought was Chase or Sam. Were they somehow trying to contact me? But why had the ghost been left in the burning rubble. Most the time I couldn't even see ghosts, unless they were ones Sam had summoned. His tended to be somewhat more corporeal.

The ghost floated into the air until it was at eye level with me, then darted past.

Alexius let out a surprised yip, then darted after

it, barking as he ran.

"Follow them!" I shouted, pointing in the direction of the dog and the ghost. The others looked up from where they'd been searching, then quickly reacted, taking off in the direction Alexius had gone. I watched the dog in the distance, picked a point where I thought he'd end up, then *traveled* there. He and the ghost darted past me, and I repeated the process, hopping along across the realm as the others remained hot on our heels.

Eventually we reached the barrier that signified the end of the current realm. It spanned upward and in either direction as far as the eye could see, and looked a bit like green jello, except I couldn't see anything on the other side. The ghost and Alexius both pressed through it without hesitation.

With a frustrated growl, I *traveled* right to the barrier then dove through it, just as everyone else reached the barrier behind me. I came out on the other side into a completely different environment. Something like a jungle.

Tall palm trees and other tropical plants lined a narrow road. The sun was hot on my face. Sweat beaded on my forehead and dripped down my temples. I searched around frantically for Alexius as everyone came up behind me.

"Got his scent," Lela stated, then ran off through the foliage.

We all followed her, though everyone soon outpaced me. I wanted to travel ahead, but I couldn't see far enough through the trees. The view would only allow me to travel in ten foot increments, so it was just as fast for me to run.

I barreled through the trees, following the sound of everyone running ahead of me, slowly leaving me behind. It was that distance that startled me when I nearly collided with Jason's back.

Recovering, I started to speak, but he whipped around and clamped a hand over my mouth. He lifted his free hand in a shushing gesture, then pointed.

I followed his gaze as he removed his hand from my mouth. Around twenty feet away, the treeline ended at an expansive beach. The ocean lapped at the distant shore. Lela and Dorrie stood with Alexius, surrounded by demons. At least, I assumed they were demons since we were all in the dream realm.

The men surrounding Lela and Dorrie wore black tactical clothing that bespoke the military, but I didn't recognize any of them. Jason and I were hidden by a large tropical plant, though if one of them looked hard enough, they'd spot us. As we watched, the men motioned toward a distant building I hadn't noticed before, mostly hidden within the trees further in the direction we had previously been running. The men motioned for Lela and Dorrie to start walking, and they obeyed. They had no choice, as they were sorely outnumbered.

Alexius had other ideas. Before any of the men could grab him, he fled, darting away into the trees far to the left of Jason and me.

I poised myself to rush forward and attack, but Jason suddenly crouched, grabbing my arm to drag me down beside him. I peeked around the base of the large plant, a pointy leaf pressing into my cheek, to see a few of the men scanning the foliage in our direction. I quickly ducked back behind the plant before any of them saw me.

We remained in our silent crouch for over a minute, then the men started talking again, though they were too far off for me to make out their hushed words. I peeked around the tree just in time to see them herding Lela and Dorrie toward the distant building.

Jason held a finger to his lips again, then tugged on my hand, slowly drawing me back with him.

I gave him a *what are you doing?* look, but didn't speak. I put my trust in the idea that whatever plan he'd thought up was better for Dorrie and Lela than me charging in to rescue them.

We continued creeping back until we were well hidden from sight, then we stood and ran a little further. Eventually Jason tugged on my arm to stop me.

"Those are the same people who took Lucy and everyone else," he whispered, scanning the trees around us.

I looked over my shoulder warily, worrying there might be hidden sentries scattered about. "They really can make portals then. That's the only way they could be here."

Jason nodded, then suddenly grabbed my arm and threw me to the ground on my stomach, plastering his body over mine. A second later I heard what had alerted him. Something was crashing toward us through the underbrush.

Alexius suddenly burst through the greenery and pounced on us. I let out a huge sigh of relief and pulled the dog into a hug as Jason and I sat up. With Alexius in my lap, I glanced over my shoulder in the direction of the building.

"We have to find a way to get in there," I whispered.

Jason nodded. "I agree, although it would be nice if we had some back up."

I clutched Alexius to me. "All of our back up is in that building. If we can get inside maybe we can free everyone, and we'll be able to overpower the kidnappers."

Jason eyed me somberly.

"What?" I asked, wondering why we were still sitting tight when we should have been attacking.

He cringed. "I hope everyone is in there too, but there's a very real possibility they might be . . . gone. Just because those men took Lela and Dorrie alive, doesn't mean the others have remained in that state."

I let out a long breath, trying to steady the nervous pattering of my heart. "Sam or Chase left that ghost in the previous realm for us to find," I explained. "It led us right here, so they were at least still alive when they arrived in the dream world."

Jason nodded. "I hope you're right."

Alexius let out a quiet growl. I thought maybe the ghost had returned, then I heard what had set him off. Someone else was walking through the dense jungle, close enough that we could hear their footsteps.

I patted Alexius' head, hoping it would soothe him. I wasn't sure if it worked, but he suddenly fell silent, then cocked his head as the footsteps neared.

Jason disappeared in the blink of an eye. Seconds later there was a feminine scream, then the sound of a struggle.

I pushed Alexius off my lap and scrambled to my feet in a crouch, then slowly approached the sounds of struggle. My progress was halted as Jason reappeared with a brunette woman trapped in his grasp. He stood behind her, holding her awkwardly by her elbows so that her hands stuck out away from her body. He had good reason for holding her that way, since she could slice someone open with invisible blades in the blink of an eye. I should know. I'd found out the hard way.

She glared as soon as she noticed me.

I glared right back. "You just couldn't leave well enough alone, could you?" I asked.

Nix spat at my feet. "Not while my cousin continued on living the good life, not caring that she'd trapped me in the dream realm."

I wasn't surprised by her words. In fact, I'd started suspecting things as soon as I'd found out I had demon relatives out for my blood. "So you're related to Art then, huh?"

She continued to glare at me. "He's my father."

I almost felt bad that my first thought was *I'm glad she lost her father like I lost mine*. Emphasis on the *almost.* I smiled coldly, and her glare faltered. Nix might be family, but she had *n o* idea who she was dealing with.

## Chapter 13

"You're too late," Nix taunted, still held immobile in Jason's grasp. "Your time right now would be better spent hiding from the demon council." She wore her usual uniform of torn jeans and a ratty teeshirt. If it weren't for the way her eyes nervously flicked around, she might look tough. As it was, she just looked like a scared teenager.

"Are you aware that your father is dead?" I asked, trying to catch her off guard.

Her brown eyes widened for a moment, then narrowed in suspicion. "You're lying, and even if you weren't, I wouldn't care. I barely know my father."

I shrugged. "If you say so. Where are my friends? Why were they brought here?"

"Did you not hear what I said about the demon council?" she asked, attempting to cock her hip but failing since Jason held her aloft to the point where her feet weren't entirely on the ground. "Aren't you curious about why they're after you, and about me being your cousin?"

I chuckled, feigning confidence. "You're a little late if you hoped for it to be a surprise. I already know about the plan to make me a victim of the council. I just don't understand why your *friends* would need so many werewolves to do that."

"They were abducted as part of the set up," she explained. She tried to glare over her shoulder at Jason, but he gave her a shake and she faced me again. "I don't know what they plan to do with them now, and I don't care. They've already fulfilled what they promised me."

I crossed my arms impatiently. "Who is this *they*?"

She smiled and shook her head. "I've said all I have to say."

I shrugged like it didn't matter. "Well then, you're of no further use to me, so I fear I must dispose of you."

Her eyes widened.

I made a fireball in my hand, then glanced past Nix to Jason. "Hold her still, would you? I wouldn't want to miss."

She started struggling, but to no avail. A relatively weak demon was no match for a vampire who was over one hundred years old. Not unless she managed to get her hands free.

"W-wait," she stammered. "I can tell you more."

I extinguished the fireball and motioned for her to continue.

"The people who have your friends call themselves *The Association*. They're all demons who were outcast from the city, either for crimes, or simply because they weren't powerful enough to survive amongst the greater demons. They've been gathering forces for a while. That's how we found them."

"And what do they want all of the werewolves for?"

She shrugged. "They were only supposed to take a few of the ones close to you, to make it look like it was your fault. Then they just kept taking them. I went with a few times, but lately they've just been leaving me here. I've been exploring the dream realms trying to find another way back."

I raised an eyebrow at her. "So I did see you at the RV park fire?"

She snorted. "I started it."

"Hmph," I replied, wondering what I should do next. I had a fleeting thought to report *The Association* to the demon council, but I couldn't risk it. If they decided to arrest me, I wouldn't be able to help my friends.

I stared at Nix, wondering what I should do with her now, then had a sudden idea. She couldn't *travel,* so if I put her somewhere else, it would take her awhile to get back to us. I took a step toward her.

She flinched and shut her eyes, the tough girl act completely gone. I really should have killed her for all the trouble she'd put me through, but I just couldn't bring myself to hate her. She'd grown up with little, and the world and our family had made her who she was. Instead of anger, I felt pity.

I grabbed her shoulder, careful to avoid her hands, then nodded to Jason.

Deducing what I planned to do, he let go as Nix and I became encased in red smoke. We landed near the bus depot. Before Nix could react, I hopped out of reach, then pictured the place where I'd left Jason. I caught a single glimpse of Nix's outraged expression, then I was standing back in the quiet jungle.

Alexius wagged his tail as soon as he saw me.

"Where'd you leave her?" Jason asked curiously.

"Bus depot," I explained. "It's several planes away from the one with the black goo. It will take her days to walk back here."

Jason nodded, seemingly satisfied with my explanation. "I'll go scout out the building," he explained. "See if I can find an unguarded entrance."

I nodded, and just like that, he was gone. Suddenly not knowing what to do with myself, I crouched down to conceal myself fully in the vegetation and placed a hand on Alexius. He let out a low growl that startled me, until I realized what he was looking at. The little ghost had returned.

Ignoring Alexius, it floated toward me, then hovered a few feet from my face, as if beckoning me.

"I can't follow you right now," I whispered, not knowing if it could understand me. Unlike my grandmother's ghost, this one was likely just composed of residual energy. The soul and personality of who it had been were long since gone.

It continued to hover, then a voice sounded in my ear, "Xoe?"

I jumped so high that I nearly knocked Alexius over. I whipped my gaze around to see if someone had approached me, but it was just me, Alexius, and the ghost.

"Xoe, are you there?" the voice said again, and I realized I recognized it. Chase was somehow speaking to me, but his voice sounded distorted and far away.

"Yes?" I whispered hesitantly.

The ghost bobbed in the air, as if nodding. "That must mean you're in the dream realm," Chase's oddly contorted voice said. "I'm in some sort of holding cell by myself. I've been able to communicate with Sam, but none of the others have responded to me. Maybe only demons can interact with my ghosts."

I kept my gaze on the ghost in front of me, amazed with how Chase was using it. "The kidnappers took Dorrie and Lela," I explained. "Jason is here with me. He's looking for a way in."

"Just the two of you?" Chase gasped. "You need to go and get backup. It's been difficult to discern from within my cell, but there have to be at least twenty demons in here, and a few vampires too."

"There is no more backup to be had," I whispered. "We figure if we can release everyone then we'll be able to outnumber them."

"If everyone is still here," Chase countered. "It may just be me and Sam. They may have had other plans for the wolves."

I bit my lip, wishing I'd grilled Nix for more information. Maybe I could go find her . . . I shook my head. No. We needed to act now, before it was too late.

"Can you tell me anything about the facility?" I pressed. "It would be nice to avoid any guards until we find you."

Chase sighed. "I was unconscious when they led me in. I haven't seen anything except the inside of this cell. Xoe, I think you should go back to the underground and look for help. Maybe the demon council will back you up."

I sighed, "No, I don't think so." I relayed everything Nix had told me. "The demon council isn't going to be any help in this," I finished. "And I'm not going to risk getting arrested and leaving everyone here."

Jason suddenly reappeared at my side, startling me. "Are you talking to that ghost?" he whispered.

I glanced at him. "It's Chase," I explained.

He raised both his eyebrows and stared at the ghost.

"I mean he's using the ghost to speak to me," I clarified. "He's being held in a cell, and so is Sam, but he hasn't been able to communicate with anyone else."

Jason nodded, comprehending the situation. "I found a way in that seems relatively unguarded. We'd only need to take down one demon to get in. It's unfortunate that Lela and Dorrie were caught, else there'd likely be no guard at all. I'm sure they're not really worried about being bothered hidden away in this realm."

I nodded and stood. "Let's go."

"Xoe!" Chase whispered harshly. "I don't think this is a good idea."

"Sit tight," I replied, ignoring his warning.

"We'll be there soon."

Jason nodded to me, then led the way back toward the compound, taking a roundabout way that would keep us deep in the trees until we reached it. Alexius followed silently behind us. I wished I could put him somewhere safe, but there were no safe places anymore, not with the demon council looking for me.

Jason crept silently ahead of me while I did my best to emulate his example. Unfortunately, I'm nowhere near as graceful as a vampire. If we got caught, I'd grab Jason and Alexius to portal out of there. We'd find somewhere safe to regroup before trying again.

It took us roughly fifteen minutes to reach the building. Sweat dripped off my brow and down my back. I wiped my palms on my jeans, but it didn't seem to make them any less clammy.

Finally, the sterile metal building came into view, and the entrance Jason had found. As he'd said, there was only one demon standing guard, a middle aged man with a fit physique, wearing the same black tactical clothing as all the rest. The only thing he was missing was a rifle in his hands, but most demons didn't need rifles. We were more dangerous without them.

Jason held out his hand and motioned for me to stop, then continued creeping forward without me. It was a good plan. Jason's stealth outmatched mine. He was more likely to take out the guard before he could sound an alarm, but it was still difficult to wait and watch. Especially with my heart threatening to escape through my throat.

Luckily the encounter took mere seconds. Jason appeared near the guard like a flash of lightning. Normally he would have put him in a chokehold to deprive him of oxygen, or he would have knocked him out, but this time he snapped his neck. I cringed and shut my eyes. It was necessary, I told myself. If we'd left the guard alive to regain consciousness, he could end up being the difference in whether we escaped or not.

Jason dragged the body away from the entrance to hide in the bushes, then returned to me.

"Sorry you had to see that," he muttered.

I nodded, but couldn't quite find my words. Instead I patted his arm, silently letting him knew he'd made the right choice.

With Alexius in tow, we crept toward the door. I was nervous that the dog would bark at an inopportune time, but he seemed to realize we were supposed to be sneaking. He silently remained glued to my side.

We reached the heavy metal door to find it locked. The building spanned out in either direction, all done in dark metal, like an impenetrable spaceship. Not wanting to take the time to search the dead guard for a key, I melted the metal doorknob off. Seconds later, I was able to swing the door outward. I took a quick peek inside to find an empty, bare-bones hallway.

"I'll go first," Jason whispered in my ear. "I'll try to disable the guards one by one until we find the others, but if there are multiple guards together, I will likely need your help."

I nodded and forced an emotionless expression. *Help* meant killing more demons, but I would do what I had to do to save my friends. "Let's go," I whispered.

Jason crept down the dimly lit hallway ahead of me. The inside of the building looked more like a warehouse than a fortress, with naked beams lining the ceiling and cheap drywall covering the walls. I followed behind Jason, stepping lightly on the concrete floor. Unfortunately, Alexius wasn't quite as adept at stealth. His toenails clicked lightly on the hard surface with every step.

Jason must have heard something, because he gestured for me to halt. He crept around a bend in the hall, then there was another sickening snap. I cringed. I knew Jason enjoyed killing even less than I did. He was going against his own morals so that I wouldn't have to.

I slowly made my way around the bend to find him stuffing the guard, another older man, into a supply closet. Once the grisly task was completed, he offered me an uneasy smile, then continued forward.

It felt like we were creeping through the hallways for hours, or maybe even days. Realistically it was maybe only five minutes, but I felt like at any moment we would be caught, and it would all be over.

The hallway ahead of us forked off in either direction. We paused at the intersection, then heard voices and footsteps coming our way. I grabbed the first doorknob I reached and ducked inside, praying the room would be empty. Jason and Alexius hurried in behind me.

I let out a sigh of relief as I leaned against the wall. Another supply room, this time filled with crates and boxes of food and water. I had the sudden urge to destroy it all out of spite, but then shook my head. It wouldn't do any good. Our mission was to get the others out, and kill the portal making demon . . . and maybe burn the building to the ground, destroy it with explosives, or find a giant bulldozer to use. I wasn't picky.

We waited quietly while the voices passed right by the door. It sounded like two more men. We probably could have taken them, but when stealth was the goal, the fewer confrontations, the better.

We waited another minute until the voices could no longer be heard. I hadn't made out much of what they were saying, but I did hear the demon council mentioned.

Jason turned his gaze to me and I nodded. He opened the door, and we both slipped back out into the hall, heading in the direction the men had come from. Hopefully they'd just finished checking on the prisoners, and we'd find them all soon.

The hallway branched off several more times as we traveled, with nary a guard in sight.

I passed by a dimly lit room with its door slightly ajar, but something had caught my eye. I backpedaled and took a peek inside, then nearly screamed when Jason appeared at my shoulder.

"I hear the buzz of electronics," he whispered, "but I don't think anything living is in the room."

I nodded, feeling like we were being insanely loud, then pushed open the door. The lights were off in the room, but it was illuminated by multiple computer screens mounted on the far wall. Underneath the screens was a massive desk that could seat three people, covered with wires and little electronic boxes. A few pairs of headphones hung from hooks at the edge of the desk.

"Looks like our suspicions about our phones being monitored were correct," Jason whispered, glancing behind us to make sure no one was approaching. "It's not important now. We should go."

I nodded, wishing I could take the time to destroy the equipment, but Jason was right. We needed to stick to our mission.

We made our way back into the quiet hall and kept walking.

A few times shouts and hurried footsteps sounded above us, as if some sort of chaos was ensuing on the second story. I kept waiting for the shouts to draw near as men hurried down the stairs to capture us, but it didn't happen. Something else was happening up there, hopefully entirely coincidental to our presence.

As we continued further down the hall, we were once again encased in silence, save the clicking of Alexius' nails.

Just when I was about to suggest we try a different route, Jason halted suddenly. I thought that he'd heard something, but then he looked over his shoulder at me and tapped his nose. *Wolves,* he mouthed.

I knew his sense of smell wasn't as keen as a werewolf, but if he said he smelled our friends, then I believed him. He continued onward, taking a right at the next turn in the hall, which lead to wide concrete stairs, leading downward.

We quickly descended, though the lighting became almost non-existent as we reached the dark bowels of the building. A foul scent reached my nostrils. The smell of unwashed bodies and other less pleasant things. I could hear someone pacing, someone wearing heavy boots. Not likely a prisoner. If there was only one guard we'd be lucky. Unfortunately, I'm rarely lucky.

All we could see from the stairs of the dimly lit space was the water-stained concrete floor ahead of us. On the last step, Jason leaned out ever so slightly to catch a glimpse of the room, then ducked back into hiding. He turned back to me and held up three fingers. Three guards.

I nodded in comprehension, then he held up two fingers and pointed right, then one, and pointed left. As far as I could guess, it meant the room branched off in either direction with two guards on one end and one on the other. He pointed to himself, then pointed right. I nodded again.

Jason motioned for me to move up to his side. I stepped lightly, cringing as Alexius' nails clacked behind me.

"What was that?" a voice asked, presumably one of the guards on the right.

Suddenly Jason was in motion and it was all I could do to scramble after him. We had to get to the guards before they could alert anyone else to our presence.

I took a sharp left, pressing my back against the wall in case my guard had anything to hurl at me. It was a worthwhile tactic, since a knife went flying right past my face. Taking only a second to recognize that the guard I faced was a woman with long red hair, I threw a fireball at her face, hoping the impact would keep her from screaming.

It didn't.

She dropped to the floor wailing in agony. I grabbed the knife that had clattered to the floor and rushed forward, quickly silencing her. I let the bloodied knife drop with a shaky hand, feeling sick to my stomach. Barely breathing, I turned around and saw two stilled bodies at Jason's feet.

"Someone will have heard her scream," he said hurriedly. "Let's get everyone out of the cells."

It was only then that I noticed the dark cells bordering either side of the room. The cells were comprised of three concrete walls, with a face of thick, steel bars.

Most of the cells on my side were empty, save for pools of blood and other fluids I didn't want to think about. All I knew was that I was glad for the darkness, robbing the blood of its vibrant color. My observation ended with only two cells that were occupied. I vaguely recognized their occupants as Vernon and Maria, two of Iva's wolves.

Each of them watched me in horror as I approached Maria's cell. Ignoring their fright, I melted the lock and opened the steel barred door of the cell, freeing Maria. She just stood there, as if not sure of my intentions. I slipped to Vernon's cell, listening for footsteps or voices, fearing more guards would approach. I melted the lock and opened the door.

Vernon looked hesitant too. I motioned with my hand for each of them to come out. They stepped nervously out of their cells and into the dim, overhead light. Maria looked like she hadn't eaten in weeks. Her olive skin was sickly pale, and her dark hair hung in clumps. Vernon had probably never looked healthy, judging by his sagging belly, but he looked near death now, nothing like the photo I'd seen of him. Both wore matching white tee shirts and white cotton pants. Yellow bruises covered the bends of their elbows, like they'd had blood taken on a regular basis.

"Stay with us," I whispered. "We're going to find the rest of the prisoners and bust out of here."

Both silently nodded with visible relief on their faces.

I glanced at Jason near the other row of cells across from us. He had three prisoners out of their cells, and a key ring in one of his hands, proffered from one of the guards. One wolf at his side was Jessica. The other two, a man and a woman, I didn't recognize.

"I swear I heard something," a voice floated down from the stairs.

Jason held a finger up to his lips, signaling for everyone to be quiet, though we didn't need much prompting. Eyeing the bloody knife on the floor where I'd dropped it, a few feet away, I stepped ever so lightly and knelt to it. Nestling it in my palm, I quietly rose, cringing as Alexius began to sniff my victim's charred face.

Two sets of footsteps echoed down the stairs moments before two more guards came into view, both men, both ridiculously muscled. They didn't stand a chance.

The werewolves in the room swarmed them like rabid animals. Jessica's fingers were tipped with long claws, a sign that she was a fairly powerful werewolf to be capable of a partial change. Jason and I didn't even have a chance to step forward before the two guards were dead, though the effort seemed to have taken a major toll on the weakened prisoners as they huffed with exertion. With how they all looked, I was surprised they were even still standing.

They all turned away from the dead guards and looked to either me or Jason, just as shouts sounded above us. Reinforcements were on their way. Goody.

## Chapter 14

"Do any of you know where the rest of the prisoners are?" I asked quickly, glancing around the cell-lined room for a second exit.

Just as my eyes landed on a door at the far end of the room past Jason, Maria pointed to it. "I've seen the guards carrying food that way," she said, her voice trembling.

"Good enough," I muttered, hustling past everyone toward the door.

No more guards had descended the stairs. They probably realized they had intruders and were developing a strategy, though their distant chaotic shouts still confused me, almost as if they didn't know just where we were and there were other things going on within the building. Not taking the time to think about it, I continued toward the door, then threw it open as I reached it. I instantly jumped back as I realized two more guards had just been preparing to charge through from their end.

We all stared at each other for a handful of seconds, then one threw a fireball at us, shocking me. I darted out of the way just in time, but the fireball hit Vernon instead.

He cried out and fell to the ground, his thigh

smoldering with flames in a fist-sized circle. His body began writhing. I'd seen the writhing before. He was about to transform into a wolf.

I glanced at the offender. I didn't often meet other fire demons. Too bad this one was trying to kill us.

Bloody dagger still in hand, I snapped back into motion and lashed at the fire demon, hoping to distract him before he could attack again. Jason whooshed by me to tackle the other guard, pinning him to the floor.

The metal knife hilt warmed in my hand. The fire demon was trying to use it to burn me, but it didn't work like he'd expected. I felt the warmth, but couldn't be burned. I smiled at him, then threw a fireball with my free hand, intending only to put him on the defensive. He fell to the ground and rolled out of the way.

There was a feminine scream somewhere behind me. More guards must have finally been coming down.

"Watch our backs!" I shouted as I dove to the ground, tumbling across the floor as the fire demon I'd been fighting threw another flaming ball at me.

My shoulder braced against the concrete floor, I threw one back at him, which he easily dodged. Luckily, Jason had dispatched his guard, and tackled the fire demon. "Get everyone out of the cells!" he shouted, then growled in pain as the fire demon latched onto his arms and began to burn him. The demon stood and backpedaled away from Jason.

I instinctively hurled the knife at the fire

demon's back. It landed in his flesh with a meaty *thunk.* As he fell away, Jason reached out and grabbed his neck, snapping it. I registered the burns on Jason's forearms, figuring he'd live, then rushed to the nearest cell. Devin was inside, wearing the same white pajama-like outfit as the others.

I melted his lock then moved on as Jason joined the fighting in the other room. The next cells held Chris, Iva, and Lucy, all wearing the same white outfits. I wanted to wrap Lucy up in a hug as I found her, but there was no time.

"Where are the others?" I asked her as Devin and the others I'd freed went to join the fighting.

"I don't know," she said weakly. "I don't even know if they're still alive. Matt is dead, and two of Iva's wolves too."

"Chase is still alive," I breathed, "he contacted me."

Lucy seemed momentarily relieved, then her eyes grew wide as the majority of the fighting moved into the current room. Guards swarmed forward, all wearing matching black clothing. How many of them were there?

I frantically searched around the room for another way out, and was rewarded with a staircase leading back to the upper level.

"Let's go," I said to Lucy, just as the fighting abruptly ended, the guards overcome by the fury of the wolves.

Alexius trotted up to my side, his mostly white fur speckled with blood to complement his black spots. I sighed with relief, glad to see he was unharmed. I quickly scanned the room for the rest of our team. One of the prisoners Jason had originally released was dead, as was Maria. Vernon was still in wolf form, slowly limping toward us. I fought back tears. More would probably die before we got out of here.

Not wanting to wait for even more guards, I jogged toward the stairs, then quickly ascended them, followed by Lucy and Jason, then everyone else still able to run. At the top of the stairs I reached a hallway branching off in either direction. There was no sign of guards, but I had a sneaking suspicion they would be waiting no matter which direction I chose. The entire compound had to be aware of our presence by now.

Jason hovered over me as I was momentarily paralyzed with indecision. Should I send the others toward the exit and just continue on with Jason, or should I risk more lives to find everyone else?

I shook myself back into reality as Devin pushed forward to stand at my side. "I smell wolves in this direction," he explained, already walking away.

I jogged to catch up with him as Jason and the others followed. We didn't have to travel for long before we found another staircase leading downward.

Jason went first, creeping down to the bottom of the stairs. He peeked around the corner of the stairwell, then hopped back as a gunshot echoed through the room. The bullet zinged right past his face to embed itself in the wall of the stairwell. All of the remaining wolves and Alexius halted behind me.

I took a few steps down and stared at the bullet hole in the wall, feeling oddly shocked. I'd never been shot at before. Although I supposed they were aiming for Jason, but I'd be next if I went into that room.

"Come out slowly!" someone called from within the lower room. "If anybody tries to attack us, we'll start killing prisoners!"

"We can't surrender," Lucy whispered from somewhere behind me. "They'll kill us all anyway."

I looked to Jason to see what he thought, but he simply shook his head. We had to make a decision. If we just remained in the stairwell, they would eventually come to capture us.

I took another step down, avoiding the final step where I'd be in the guard's line of fire. Just like the other room, I couldn't see much, except for the concrete floor, and what looked like a trash can full of blood stained rags. Trying not to think too hard about whose blood was on the rags, I reached out my hand and concentrated. A moment later, the rags burst into flame.

"What the-" one of the guards began.

"It must be Alexondre's daughter," the other guard guessed. "She's a fire demon just like her dad."

It was odd, for some reason I felt like these demons weren't overly concerned with the plot against me. Like the fact that I was there was entirely secondary to whatever else was going on. They almost seemed surprised that I would even come to rescue the wolves at all. What else were they doing out in the dream world jungle, and why did they want so many werewolves?

The burning rags began to emit acrid smoke to slowly fill the room. Someone within coughed, but it was a weak cough, like the smoke was hitting the prisoners before it reached the guards.

"A flaming trash can isn't going to do it!" one of the guards called.

I glanced up the stairwell toward my waiting comrades. There'd been no signs that we were going to be ambushed from behind, but I still didn't like remaining there for the guards to make the next move.

I turned back to see the smoke continuously billowing out of the trashcan, even though the flames had died down. The smoke might obscure us a bit from whoever had the gun, but not enough.

Jason touched my arm. "I'll go," he whispered. "I can probably get the gun away from him before he fires."

I bit my lip, not liking the suggestion. We hadn't come across any yet, but we knew there were vampires working with the demons. If a vampire held the gun, he'd be just as fast as Jason.

"I'll try to distract them," I assured.

As Jason prepared to run out, I crouched down on the second to last step. Whoever had the gun would likely aim around chest height if someone appeared, so I'd just have to take my chances and stay as low as possible. I summoned a fireball into my hand, wanting to be able to throw it before the guards could react.

I nodded to Jason, then we both dove out into the hall. I landed on my shoulder, sending a jolt of pain through my body as I threw the fireball. It went wide, missing both guards, but they'd been momentarily distracted. The next thing I knew, Jason was standing behind the guard with the handgun. He reached out to snap the guard's neck, just as the unarmed guard, a boy that couldn't have been more than sixteen with bright red hair, turned. Before he could act, I hurled another fireball at him. At the same time, the armed guard's neck emitted a sickening snap.

The red-haired kid screamed, frantically attempting to pat out the fire eating up his clothing and the skin beneath. Jason tried to grab him, but he fell to the ground and rolled away toward me. I prepared to react, but had no time. Everyone else had streamed into the hallway behind us. Devin caught the kid and quickly slit his throat with a dagger he must have apprehended from a guard.

I looked down at the boy's bloody, burned body, and felt suddenly ill. He was probably younger than me. Had he been a part of the whole scheme, or was he just following orders? Maybe his dad was another guard, and his son had only been trying to gain his approval.

I halted my spiraling thoughts. The guards were all accomplices to whatever was going on in the hidden compound. They were *all* responsible for the wolves who'd died so far. I steeled my expression and looked up to Jason, but he was busy shuffling through another key ring proffered from the guards.

I moved to his side, hoping Chase was in one of

the cells, but I knew he wasn't. Jason would have said something. Two cells held unknown prisoners, likely more werewolves. I quickly melted the locks, working things out in my mind. We now had acquired four wolves that weren't in Iva's file. Though several wolves had been killed since we started, it was still odd that they'd been here at all. That meant wolves were being collected that had nothing to do with us. What were they doing with them?

The newly rescued prisoners had healing bruises at the bends of their elbows, just like those I'd initially noticed on Vernon and Maria. I shook my head. No time to think about it. We needed to find the others.

There were no other doors in the room, so we'd have to go back up the stairs. At least I was starting to understand the layout of the building, the current portion anyway. There was a long hall on the upper floor, branching off to other parts of the building, with sets of staircases leading down into the small, cell-lined rooms. Though each room had eight to ten cells, so far they'd each only held a few prisoners. Had they all been filled at one point? Lucy said Matt had died before we got there. How many others had perished?

Jason touched my arm to bring me back to reality, then gestured to the stairs. He was covered in blood, his tee shirt torn in multiple spots. I nodded numbly, and we both led the way back to the upper hallway. All was silent around us, save for our footsteps and those of the wolves that followed. I knew there had to be other guards in the compound, but none had presented themselves. What were they planning, and where were Sam, Chase, and Allison?

I was so deep in my thoughts as we walked down the hall that I almost didn't notice that the little ghost had rejoined us. It bobbed in front of my face as we walked.

"Chase?" Jason questioned, halting beside me to stare at the ghost.

I nodded. "I think so."

The ghost floated a few feet ahead of us, then bobbed beside a closed door.

"That's in the opposite direction of the lower level," Jason commented. "There are likely still others to be released from their cells."

I considered the ghost, knowing it would likely lead me to Chase, though he hadn't attempted to speak through it this time.

I turned my gaze to Jason, taking in his blood splattered shirt and face, and his grime soaked jeans and shoes. I had already put him through hell, and now I was going to have to ask for a little more. "You take the others to inspect the remaining cells. I'll follow the ghost."

"We shouldn't split up," he argued.

I glanced at the ghost again, then back to him. "I don't know what the people here are planning, but we need to get everyone together ASAP. I'll take Lucy and Devin. You take everyone else."

He sighed. "I'd tell you to be careful if I thought you'd listen."

I smiled. "Careful will be my new middle name."

"Good," he breathed. "I was getting tired of *Trouble*."

He gripped my arm for a moment, then continued down the hall. I watched the other wolves as they passed, leaving Devin and Lucy behind with me. Alexius ran off after Jason and the others, and I didn't try to stop him. He'd probably be safer with those freeing the wolves from the cells than with me, wherever I was going.

"Did Chase really send that ghost?" Lucy asked. She had less blood on her than everyone else, but still looked ready for a fight.

"Yes," I replied, "and I think it will lead us to him, and hopefully Sam. When Chase was able to communicate with me, he explained that he could also communicate with Sam, but neither of them had seen anyone else. I think they're being held some place more private than the cells."

"We should hurry up and find them," Devin interrupted. "I don't like standing out in the open like this."

I nodded in agreement, then turned and jogged to where the ghost waited. I tried the knob on the door to find it locked, but was able to make short work of it. I was getting tired though. Between portals and fireballs, I'd used up a lot of my energy.

I pulled the door outward to reveal another staircase, this time leading upward. I paused to listen, but didn't hear anything above the well-lit corridor. With a nod to Devin and Lucy, I ascended the stairs, stepping lightly, wary that more guards might have guns.

I reached the top and opened another door, unlocked this time. I entered a large white room with Lucy and Devin following close behind me. The room looked like it belonged in a hospital. The walls and floor were a perfect, sterile white. There were few pieces of furniture save steel cabinets and shelves lining the walls. An area to our left had several large refrigerators with clear glass doors. They were all entirely filled with vials of blood. I glanced back at Devin and Lucy, who both stared at the vials with distaste.

"They've been taking it since we got here," Lucy explained. "That's how Matt died. He was in a cell across from me and they took too much."

I thought of Matt's smiling face and light-hearted demeanor and felt suddenly ill. If only we'd figured things out sooner, we might have been able to save him.

I took a shaky breath and looked around for the ghost. It was bobbing by another door on the side of the room opposite the stairs. I approached it, and peeked inside through a small glass window set into the heavy steel of the door. I quickly ducked away. Several armed guards were within. If Chase was somewhere in there, it would explain why he hadn't spoken through the ghost again. Didn't want to get shot.

My back pressed against the wall next to the door, I gestured for Lucy and Devin to join me. Since the guards obviously hadn't heard us speaking, I wagered that the walls and door were soundproof, but still I lowered my voice to a whisper as I explained the situation to my companions.

They exchanged worried looks, then turned back to me.

"What should we do?" Lucy whispered. "If we barge in there, the guards might shoot Chase."

"Or *us*," Devin added. "We need some sort of distraction."

The ghost came to bob in front of my face again, as if trying to tell me something. As I tried to deduce what the ghost wanted, an eerie feeling permeated my bones, raising goosebumps on my arms. The wall behind me grew cold to the touch.

"I think our distraction is happening right now," I whispered.

I crept back toward the door and angled myself for a quick peek through the viewing window. With the longer glance I counted five guards, all shifting around nervously. They glanced around the room and over their shoulders, as if expecting a sudden attack. I ducked back down out of view before one of them could see me.

Crouching below the door, I closed my eyes and tried to sense what was going on in the room. The eerie feeling was growing, similar to what I felt when I visited graveyards, but amplified. The energy was building toward . . . something.

I stood and risked another quick peek into the room. It had filled with fog, almost too thick to see anything. I briefly considered waiting for the guards to run out so we could launch a surprise attack, but dismissed the idea. If they were going to run, they would have already done it, and I didn't want them to catch on and shoot Chase.

I gave Devin and Lucy a quick nod, then flung open the door. I instantly dropped into a crouch as a gun fired, then I dove for the nearest set of legs. I burned them with as much force as I could during the momentary contact, then rolled away as another gun sounded. The room erupted into a cacophony of gunshots and grunts of pain as Lucy and Devin joined the fray.

The struggle didn't last long, and I realized the men were armed for a reason. They were human. They hadn't stood a chance against us. What the hell were humans doing working with demons in the dream world?

Once all of the guards were either dead or otherwise incapacitated, the fog cleared, revealing Lucy and Devin. Lucy clutched her shoulder where blood was blossoming on her white shirt. She'd been shot.

My eyes widened as I took a step toward her.

"It's fine," she rasped through gritted teeth, "let's find Chase."

Devin moved to another steel door, much like the one we'd come through to enter the room. "In here," he instructed.

I moved to Devin's side and peered through the window. Chase sat in the corner of an empty room, his hands bound behind his back. What I could see of his face was covered in bruises, though the angle at which he slumped hid his eyes.

I tried the handle on the door. It was locked. I melted it, but more slowly than the others, due to its thickness. Had the kidnappers felt a demon needed better security than the werewolves, or had they simply known he would have been one of my priorities, and wanted to keep me away from him?

After several excruciating seconds, the door swung open, no longer held in place by the lock and handle. I rushed to Chase's side.

He looked up at me groggily. "Bout time," he muttered. "Do you know how difficult it is to distract an entire compound of armed guards?"

My eyebrows raised. "Come again?"

"After we spoke I started distracting them with my ghosts, those I could reach, anyway," he explained. "I didn't want them attacking you."

Ah, the confused shouting of the guards suddenly made sense. Chase had been sending his ghosts to mess with them, letting Jason and I slip in without facing too many guards.

I hugged him, though he winced in pain, then I slipped my hand down to find a thick plastic zip tie around his wrists. I gave it a quick burst of heat, and it melted away. I moved so he could slowly bring his arms forward. Judging by the way he moved, he'd been in that position for a while.

Once he'd recovered, he wrapped me up in his arms, ignoring the fact that I was splattered with blood, and had patches of the sticky black ooze from the other dream realm on my clothes. "I thought I'd never see you again," he whispered against my hair.

I would have liked to stay there hugging him, but Jason and the others might need our help. I pulled away. "You didn't really think you could get rid of me that easily, did you?"

He smiled, then winced. His face was more purple than flesh-toned. "Are all of the witches dead?"

"The guards outside I questioned?" I'd noticed that they were human, but hadn't realized they were witches. It made sense though, a group of witches was a good idea for guarding a demon. Magic to counteract magic. The witches were likely why Sam had been unable to travel out of his cell. Certain wards could prevent magical escape.

Devin stepped into the room and aided me in helping Chase stand. This was bad. I suspected Chase would hardly be able to walk, let alone fight. Lucy, still clutching at her shoulder, didn't look much better.

Unfortunately, we had no choice. We all hobbled out of the cell together, then out into the previous room. The moment we stepped into the white, sterile space, an entire hoard of gunmen stepped into view, all aiming at me.

## Chapter 15

"I knew you'd be troublesome," a voice said from somewhere behind the gunmen, "but I truly never thought you'd get *this* far."

"Sorry to exceed your expectations," I muttered, warily searching the row of gunmen for the source of the voice.

As if on cue, two of the armed men stepped aside, revealing a lanky man in a lab coat. Though his eyes and hair were dark brown, his features were too familiar to be brushed aside. They were features I missed dearly.

"Funny," I began, standing straight as Chase removed his arm from my shoulder to let me stand on my own, "I seem to recall finding you severely decayed with a dagger sticking out of your chest, Art."

It *had* to be Art, unless my dad had yet another brother. The similarities in appearance were too apparent.

He smirked. "So you found my decoy and the journal? Good job."

I tried to keep the surprise off my face, bluffing that I'd known the man in the tent wasn't Art all along. "Why'd you even bother planting them? I was already in Nevada like you wanted."

He straightened his lab coat and took a bold step forward, showing no fear facing down two demons and two werewolves. Of course, we were all barely still standing, and we did have guns pointed at us.

"I wanted to lure you here, of course," he explained. "If you didn't deduce that this was all orchestrated by your demon kin, you would have never figured out to look for us in the dream world."

I didn't bother to mention that we'd found the hideout by sheer happenstance. The dream world would have been the last place I looked, even knowing there was another demon who could create portals.

"Ah, so you didn't figure it out?" he asked, gazing intently at my expression, which had apparently given me away.

*Crap.* I really needed to work on my poker face.

He laughed. "I even instructed Nix to let you spot her at the RV park, so you'd know we'd been in the dream realm to fetch her. It really wasn't very nice of you to leave her there, by the way."

I glanced at the armed men. They'd been pointing their guns at me for a while. I really didn't want one of them to get jumpy and pull the trigger.

Ignoring his jibe, I glared at him. "You know if you kill me here, you won't be able to frame me with the demon council. You won't inherit my place in demon society."

He smirked. "On the contrary, placing you here is all part of the set up. We couldn't very well link you to the facility if you'd never been here. The demon council has *dreamers*. Once we clean up shop, we'll lead them here to you, where you'll be locked in a warded cell, betrayed by the people you hired to kidnap all of the wolves."

"And my motivation for kidnapping the wolves?" I inquired curiously, hoping for more information.

He glanced at the fridges full of blood. "A lucrative side business. One I will be benefitting from, once you're out of the way."

I glanced at the fridges warily, waiting for him to go on, then turned back in time to see his satisfied smile.

"Werewolf blood is worth a fortune," he explained. "Demons and witches can use it in their rituals and alchemy, and vampires will buy it. They're often looking for something with a little extra kick." He glanced past me to the room beyond where we'd killed the witches and sneered. "Unfortunately it looks like I'll need to hire new pawns to distribute the blood to the human world.

So he'd taken the extra wolves to sell their blood, and had hired a network of witchess and vampires to sell it. He was going to get rich off their deaths.

Devin stepped forward and half the guns moved to point at him. He raised his arms in an *I'm harmless* gesture, but he was also covered in the blood of the gunmen's comrades, so the act fell a little short.

Art chuckled. "Kill everyone except

Alexondra," he ordered.

"Wait," I said quickly.

He held up an arm to delay the gunmen, then raised a dark eyebrow at me. "Yes? Would you like to say your final goodbyes to your friends."

"No," I muttered, looking down at my shoes and acting cowed. I was about to take a huge risk, but I saw no other choice.

Art waited for me to continue.

Without warning, I quickly threw multiple fireballs at the fridges full of blood. They exploded, spewing red liquid and shards of glass everywhere. Taking advantage of the distraction, I used all of my remaining energy to create a dome of fire around me, Chase, Devin, and Lucy. I'd done it once before to protect some of us from my grandmother's ghostly attacks. I wasn't positive it would work on bullets, but if it could keep out pure balls of energy, it should work against more mundane attacks.

Shots fired, but the bullets didn't penetrate. They disintegrated into nothing as they hit the wall of flame. I huffed a sigh of relief.

A frustrated shout drew my attention away from the incoming bullets. Art was looking down at the remaining werewolf blood as it dripped out of the ruined carcasses of the refrigerators.

"Kill them all!" he shouted, turning his attention to us.

A shower of bullets reached the barrier and disappeared.

Art lifted an arm to cease the gunmen's fire,

then approached my barrier, rage clear on his face. "Hide in there as long as you please," he said through gritted teeth. "We'll go and kill the rest of your friends in the mean time."

I tried to feign confidence, but knew he'd caught my nervous eye flick toward the door that led to the stairwell.

He smiled cruelly, and began to walk away.

There was a sudden *bang* as the door in question flew open, slamming against the wall. "Her friends are already here," a voice said a moment later. I caught a flash of Abel's grin, then white-clothed werewolves flooded into the room, followed by several who'd assumed wolf form. In the rush I caught sight of Dorrie, her sparkly white skin speckled with blood.

More shots fired, but the gunmen were no match for the oncoming hoard. I let down my barrier and dove for Art, hoping to catch him off guard, but there was one thing I'd forgotten. *Someone* there could make portals. I found out a second later that the *someone* was Art.

His arms snapped around me and we were propelled upward. I had no time to react. A moment later we touched down on soft green grass. I could tell by the feel of the place that we were somewhere else in the dream world. That was the only thought I had before Art punched me square in the jaw.

I fell to my back in the grass, stunned. I glimpsed a cheerful blue sky, then a boot heel stomped down on my stomach, doubling me over in pain. I curled up on my side, but couldn't move any further.

"Your friends will never make it out of the dream realm!" he shouted, then kicked me in the ribs. "The only ones who can release them are you and I!"

Swallowed in pain, I could barely breathe. I tried to form a fireball, but he kicked me again and I went rolling through the grass. I heard him running up for another kick, then closed my eyes and travelled in a wash of red smoke, reappearing behind him on my feet.

I threw a fire ball at his back, but he turned and dodged it. "Of course you can travel *a n d* make portals," he growled as he began to stalk toward me.

I coughed and came up with blood. I spat a red glob into the grass and smiled weakly. "So what? You can make portals too. What do you have to complain about?"

A gentle wind ruffled the grass around us. The place would have been incredibly peaceful if there wasn't a demon trying to kill me.

Art sneered. "Don't pretend to know how difficult my life has been, and Nix's. *She* should be the one in your place with the nice house in the demon city, with no one attacking her to snuff out what little power she has."

I laughed, though it nearly doubled me over in pain. "You think I'm not attacked? That's rich."

He rushed me and I launched another fireball. It hit him in the chest, but he kept going, tackling me to the ground. Since he was a demon, I couldn't burn him by touch, so I tried to travel away.

He held on as I barely managed to dissipate, but it was too weak, and we ended up in the grass again. I'd already been on the verge of collapse back at the hidden compound, but I managed to travel one more time, though the attempt was futile. He came along for the ride again, forced me to the ground. His hands wrapped around my throat.

I flailed my arms weakly, trying to summon another fireball, but I couldn't get the correct angle to hit him. My vision began to go black as I stared at the snarling face above me.

I heard a growl, but it sounded distant, probably because of the lack of oxygen. Probably just a hallucination. My arms fell weakly to my sides. I was only seconds from passing out for good.

Suddenly the weight on top of me disappeared. My vision slowly came back in stages. I tried to move. I needed to take this opportunity to defend myself from Art, but my limbs ached with exhaustion. I'd used too much power, and now I was paying the price.

Something warm and wet slid across my face. My eyes slowly tilted to the side to see black and white fur, flecked with red.

"Were you aware your dog can make portals?" a voice asked.

I forced my head to turn to the voice, my cheek smashed on the grass. Chase was there, slumped on the ground. Alexius barked, preferring my attention to be on *him.*

"What?" I muttered, still feeling like I might be on the brink of death.

Chase lifted his head enough to meet my eyes. Art's prostrate form was sprawled in the grass beside him.

"Alexius. He came into the room with Abel and the others," Chase explained. "As soon as Art took you, Alexius began to fade from sight. Realizing what was happening, I dove for him and came along for the ride."

I tried to smile, but my face didn't seem to be working. I couldn't even feel where Art had punched me, which let me know I either had other more severe injuries, or I was in shock.

"Can you come over here?" I asked weakly.

He smiled apologetically. "Not quite sure I can move yet. That last burst of adrenaline was all I had."

Alexius yipped to get my attention. I turned my head toward him and he licked me straight on the lips.

"Ach!" I groaned, wanting to lift an arm to wipe away the slobber, but not wanting to exert the energy. I turned my face away to see Chase slowly crawling toward me. His visible skin was a mess of scrapes and bruises.

"You look like you've been tortured," I joked.

He stopped crawling, his gaze heavy upon me.

I raised my eyebrows in question. "Have you?" I asked finally.

"They wanted me to use my ghosts to lure you into a trap," he explained. "I refused."

He resumed crawling. Reaching me, he placed his hand in mine, then slumped to the ground on his back beside me. "Think you can take us back?"

202

I thought about it, but really wasn't sure. "Is Art dead?" I asked, turning my gaze up to the blue sky.

"Yeah," Chase muttered, sounding on the verge of sleep.

I closed my eyes and thought of the hidden compound, but for some reason, with the comforting sun on my face, I just kept thinking of the beach that was near it.

Moments later we ended up in the warm sand.

"This is nice," Chase muttered as Alexius appeared beside us, having traveled of his own volition.

"Good dog," I whispered. This seemed like a good place to go to sleep, but I needed to check on everyone else.

I heard footsteps in the sand a moment before a figure cast a shadow across my face. I looked up, but the sun was at the person's back, silhouetting their form in brightness. All I could make out was that the man wore a suit and sunglasses, and had dark hair.

"Alexondra Meyers?" he questioned.

"Mmhmm?" I answered. I was pretty sure Chase was unconscious beside me.

"You're a hard woman to find," the man commented.

I frowned. "Care to help me up? I need to check on my friends."

"They're fine," he assured. "You, on the other hand . . ."

At some point my eyes had drifted closed. "Is that a threat?"

He chuckled. "No, simply an observation."

"Who are you?" I asked, seriously wondering if he was a figment of my delusional imagination.

I opened my eyes a sliver as he crouched beside me. "I'm a *dreamer* employed by the demon council," he explained. "I was sent here to investigate an organization called *The Association*, though they seem to have recently disbanded."

My lips formed an *'oh'* of understanding. "Am I under arrest?"

"Should you be?" he asked.

"Nope," I muttered. "It was all a set up."

"Yes," he mused. "There's a troupe of blood spattered werewolves who I imagine will back up your story."

I heaved a sigh of relief. If he'd seen the werewolves, that meant they were probably alright.

"Rest for a while," he instructed. "You'll need your strength to transport this many people back to the human world."

"You can't do it?" I mumbled, slurring my words.

He chuckled. "I'm just a dreamer, here in an observatory capacity."

I'm pretty sure at that moment I called a member of the demon council a useless waste of space, then I slumped into comfortable oblivion.

## Chapter 16

I awoke to the smell of smoke, and numerous presences gathered around me. The sun was just beginning to set, casting the beach and surrounding jungle in shadow. I sat up in the sand to see the surviving werewolves and Sam, Allison, and Jason, all patiently waiting for me to take them back to the human world. Behind them stood everyone else, including Dorrie and Cynthia.

The nearby compound was on fire. Good riddance.

Chase slowly sat up beside me. "Is it over?" he asked.

I looked over Allison and Lucy to meet Jason's eyes. He nodded.

"Yep," I replied. "Who wants to go home?"

Everyone raised their hands, and I took a moment to count the survivors. On one side stood Jason, Lucy, Allison, and Sam. On the other were Devin, Abel, Lela, Dorrie, Cynthia, and Jessica. No Iva, or Chris. There were a few others I didn't know, but just judging by the numbers, many had died in the fight for freedom. I swallowed a lump in my throat. So many had died.

I wasn't sure if I could bring the entire group in

a portal at once, but I was about to try. I wanted to get the hell out of there, now more than ever.

"Gather around me," I instructed. "We'll all need to huddle together. Make sure everyone is holding onto someone who's holding onto someone else."

Everyone huddled around me, including Chase and Alexius. I closed my eyes, then opened them, wondering where I should take everyone.

As if sensing my predicament, Abel tightened his grip on Devin, then said, "Take us back to Shelby. We can all make our ways home from there."

I nodded, then closed my eyes again, thinking of the woods near my home. Moments later we landed, and I felt ready to pass back out again. It was nighttime, and that was all I was able to discern. I had created multiple portals, fireballs, and a shield. The last time I'd made a shield I'd been ready to pass out from that alone. I was getting stronger, but not strong enough to withstand a physical beating after using so much energy. I slumped down onto the loamy earth and couldn't move.

Someone gathered me into their arms and stood, cradling me like a child. I doubted it was Chase since he was in even worse shape than I, but I knew it was at least an ally, not an enemy. All of the enemies were dead.

I watched the moon through the canopy of pine trees as I was carried. I felt more like I was floating. My mind drifted over all that had happened. Art had organized other demons to lure me in, and to sell werewolf blood on the side. Vampires and witches had been involved too. Most of them were probably dead, though there were likely others in the human world that would need to be hunted down, and Nix was still in the dream realm. They were all a worry for another day. We were home, and we were alive . . . most of us anyway.

I felt suddenly guilty for not caring more about the other deaths. I did feel bad, but part of me was glad that no one close to me had been taken away. Chase, Lucy, Allison, Jason, Dorrie, and Lela were all still alive. My mind flitted to Dorrie and the fact that I'd brought her to the human world, but that was as far as my thoughts went. The moon shone her soft light down on me, coaxing me back to sleep. Though I'm prone to arguments, I wasn't about to argue with the moon herself, that would just be silly.

xx

I woke gasping for air as someone dragged me out of bed. A hand clamped over my mouth. I swatted against them, but was still too weak to do anything else. I registered that I was in my room at my mom's house, but if that was the case, who the heck was dragging me toward the open window?

I collapsed my knees to hinder our progress, but whoever had me didn't seem to notice. I reached out for my power and was answered with only a dull echo.

"Ergh," my captor gasped in pain.

It hadn't been much, but I'd managed to burn his arm where it wrapped around my chest. In his surprise, he dropped me and I was able to turn around and look up at him.

"Eric?" I questioned as the moonlight streaming in through the window hit his face.

His eyes were red-rimmed and puffy. He scowled at me. "Where is Iva? You said you'd bring her back with you. I drove all night and day to get here."

I froze, not knowing how to deliver the bad news.

"You said you'd save her!" he rasped, then lunged forward. He grabbed me around my neck and pushed me to the carpet. My body screamed in protest from the bruises inflicted by Art. Eric's hands compressed, squeezing my airway shut.

The door burst open and slammed against the wall. A white shape plowed into Eric, shoving him off me. I slowly regained my senses and skittered away to flip on the light. After a moment of painful blindness as my eyes adjusted, I was able to focus on Dorrie, holding Eric aloft by his throat. He sputtered, attempting to pry her fingers away, but even a vampire's strength couldn't match Dorrie for pure fury.

"She has been through *enough*," Dorrie growled into Eric's face.

I stumbled forward, sensing that Eric didn't have long to live. "Don't kill him," I rasped, still trying to catch my breath. "He's just upset because his girlfriend is dead."

Dorrie retracted her hand and Eric crumpled to the ground. He hunched over and curled into a little ball. At first I thought he was trying to catch his breath, then I realized he was crying. "You said you'd save her," he sobbed, pressing his face into his hands.

A fine trembling overcame my body, an odd mixture of retreating adrenaline, exhaustion, and guilt. I felt a presence at my back and turned to see Chase. He must have been sleeping downstairs on the couch. He peeled his gaze away from Eric to look at me, then shook his head. There was nothing we could do for the mourning vampire.

Dorrie approached and placed a hand gently on my arm.

I jumped at her touch.

"I'll watch him," she said softly. "Maybe you two should go back underground. Just don't answer the door if the demon council comes back."

My eyes widened and I sucked in a breath, realizing I hadn't told anyone about my encounter with the demon council *dreamer*. I was pretty sure Chase had been unconscious for the exchange, so unless the dreamer had spoken with the blood-spattered werewolves he'd referred to, no one else knew about the meeting.

I opened my mouth to explain, but thought better of it. I'd fill Dorrie in when there wasn't a sobbing vampire on my floor. I backed out of the room with Chase.

Once we were in the hall, he pulled me toward

him, wrapping me in a tight embrace. The pressure hurt my bruises, but I didn't care. It was worth it. I felt tears forming in my eyes. "Let's go home," I whispered.

He nodded and kissed my temple, then I closed my eyes and thought of my dad's house. There's no place like home. There's no place like home.

We appeared in my dad's kitchen, surrounded by red smoke. As I'd expected, the room was trashed. Still partially in Chase's embrace, I turned and buried my head against his chest, not wanting to look too closely at the rubble.

Seeming to sense what I needed, Chase slowly guided me out of the kitchen. Once we were in the undamaged entry room, he took my hand and led me down the hall to my bedroom. We went inside, and my tension eased an iota. The room was sparsely furnished, with no real hints that I'd entirely settled in there, but it felt like home. It felt *safe*. Even though my dad would never be there again, it was like I could sense his presence, watching over us.

Chase led me toward the bed, and we both collapsed. He flipped onto his back so I could nestle my head in the crook of his shoulder. His arm snaked underneath me to wrap around my back.

"Everything is going to be different now," I breathed, "isn't it?"

So many had died. I wasn't sure what Allison had gone through, but Lucy had been trapped in a cell where demons stole her blood. Same with Devin, and probably with Abel. Chase had been tortured because

210

of me. It had *all* happened because of me. I thought of Eric's heart-wrenching sobs and shivered. That was my fault too.

Chase turned his face to kiss my forehead. "Some things will perhaps be different, but everyone will recover."

"Will you?" I asked, my voice cracking with unshed tears.

"I'm already well on my way," he replied, "all because of you. You saved me."

"I *endangered* you," I replied instantly. "This all happened because my demon relatives wanted what I have. Everyone was caught in the crossfire because of me."

"They wanted the werewolves' blood," he countered. "It would have happened regardless."

"If I'd figured things out sooner, I could have saved everyone," I argued.

He took a deep breath, then let it out. "Don't you dare blame yourself for this. You've been targeted by demon after demon. You've been kidnapped, beaten, and you even lost your father. *None* of this is your fault."

I let out a heavy sigh. I didn't agree with him, but knew it was futile to argue.

He pulled me closer and kissed my cheek. "How about tomorrow we go fetch Dorrie, then we all relax down here and have a movie and pizza day?"

"What about the wolves?" I groaned, thinking his idea would have been perfect if it had only been possible.

"Devin and Abel already demanded that you let them take care of everything," he explained. "They know you need to rest."

"What about Eric?" I pressed.

"I imagine once he's calmed down, he'll go back home," he said softly. "Deep down he's probably blaming himself for Iva's death. That's something he's going to have to deal with on his own."

I flipped over onto my back and stared up at the dark ceiling. "Well then what about the demon council?"

Chase sighed. "Maybe now that everything has been dealt with, they will have no reason to investigate you."

Once again reminded that he'd been unconscious when the *dreamer* visited us on the beach, I took a deep breath and told him about the encounter.

"So they know *everything*?" he asked, his voice breathy with disbelief.

"Yeah," I sighed. "Which is good in the sense that I probably won't be blamed for the wolves that didn't make it, especially since Abel is around to back me up, but the dreamer made it seem like I'd still have to answer to the council as a whole."

He pulled me close again. "We'll deal with it when it happens. *If* it happens."

I nodded, finally starting to feel a measure of relaxation. "So we really don't have anything we *have* to do tomorrow?"

"Nope," he replied. "Except maybe clean the

kitchen up a bit."

I returned to my side and buried my face against his neck. Neither of us had showered since our ordeal, but I didn't care. After almost losing him, almost losing *everyone*, I was just overwhelmingly grateful that most of us made it out alive. I'd need to talk to Jason, to thank him for all that he did for me, but that could wait until we'd all physically recovered. He'd had to kill a lot of people, and I knew it would be weighing on him, just as it was weighing on me. The emotional recovery would take a little longer, and I owed it to him to do all that I could to help.

I would need to visit Allison and Lucy too. I wasn't sure what had been done to Allison, but Lucy had suffered the equivalent of torture. She'd need a friend. Sam would also likely need a bit of coddling, but I'd leave that up to Chase. I was pretty sure after everything, Chase would be seeing his brother in a new light, and would maybe deign to give him a true second chance.

I inhaled and let out a long breath as the rest of my tension eased away. We'd all be there for each other as much as we each needed. After all, that's what families are for.

## Chapter 17

Chase, Dorrie, and I all lounged on the couch in our pajamas, arguing about which movie we were going to watch first. I didn't *really* care. I was just glad to be curled up next to Chase, with Alexius sleeping soundly near our feet.

A knock sounded on the front door, interrupting our argument.

"Pizza!" I exclaimed, then bounded from the couch to jog down the hall toward the front door. I was still nursing a few bruises from the beating Art had given me, but I'd recovered my energy, at least enough that running to answer the door wasn't a struggle.

I reached the front door and opened it happily, then almost shut it again. Outside stood five demons in black suits with matching black sunglasses. They all had short hair cuts and exhibited a feeling of sameness, though the group possessed a variety of complexions.

"I'm guessing you guys aren't here to deliver our pizza?" I asked weakly. Feeling suddenly woefully underdressed, I tugged my short white tee shirt to cover the sliver of my belly that was showing. Unfortunately, there was nothing to be done for my baggy plaid pajama pants and bare feet.

One of the men with dark hair and skin smirked, then handed me an official-looking document. I gingerly took it from his hand and looked down to read it as Chase appeared behind me.

A few moments later, I glanced up. "A pardon from the demon council?"

One of the other men nodded. "In exchange for a favor."

I frowned, then re-read the page, which basically excused me from a myriad of crimes, some of which I'd actually committed. "It doesn't say anything about a favor," I commented, my eyes remaining on the paper.

The man who'd originally handed me the pardon cleared his throat. "We prefer for such things to remain unrecorded." He seemed almost . . . embarrassed?

"What's the favor?" I asked.

The man now seemed relieved. "While you're aware that we have *dreamers* in our employ, we do not have any demons capable of making portals to the dreamworld. A few members of *The Association* still linger in the dream realm, but without their leader, are trapped there."

"*And?*" I asked, implying that we should just leave them there.

The men let out a collective sigh. "*Someone* must stand trial for all that has occurred. If you will agree to collect them, that someone will not be you, except to serve as a witness to their crimes."

216

I bit my lip, looked down at the paper again, then held out my free hand. "Deal."

No one took my hand to shake it. Instead, they all turned to glare at the pizza delivery guy walking up the path behind them.

They all turned back to me as one. "We'll be in touch to supply the details of where you should deliver the prisoners," one explained. "Once this task is done, we can perhaps even overlook the *driver* living in your home."

I blanched, wondering just how long they'd known about Dorrie, or if they'd only just discovered her existence when we'd dealt with *The Association.*

The men turned and walked away without a goodbye, and the pizza man nervously crept forward. He was probably around sixteen with bright red hair, reminding me of the young demon we'd killed in the hidden compound.

"Were those men with the demon council?" he whispered as he handed me the pizza.

I nodded and set my *pardon* on top of the pizza box as I took it in hand.

Chase stepped forward to pay.

The kid looked between the two of us nervously, then settled on me. "What did you do?" he asked bravely.

I smirked and lifted a brow at him. "What *didn't* I do?"

He gasped, then quickly backed away, payment in hand.

I handed the pizza to Chase, then shut the door

and leaned against it.

Chase grinned at me.

"What's so funny?" I asked tiredly.

He leaned down to kiss me on the cheek, then took the pizza from my hands, leaving me with the pardon. "You have no idea how lucky we just got."

I stared up at him. "Explain."

"The council messed up," he began as we both moved away from the door to return to the den where Dorrie was waiting. "They should have caught on to *The Association* sooner, and should have taken care of it themselves. That pardon," he glanced down at the piece of paper still in my hand, "is their way of covering their butts. You did their job for them, so they're letting everything slide. My guess is they would have given you the pardon even without the *favor*, but since you're the only one capable of retrieving the stragglers in the dream realm, they were forced to ask."

"Huh," I replied, not sure what else to say.

We re-entered the den. Dorrie was standing nervously by the back wall, as if prepared to flee. She held Alexius by his collar, obviously intending to take him into hiding with her.

"Was that the council, Dumpling?" she whispered. "Do I need to hide?" Alexius tilted his head at us, clearly asking the same question.

I grinned at her. "Nope, we have an official pardon. They know about you, and you get to stay."

She dropped the dog's collar then barreled into me for a painful hug. I flailed my arms and beseeched

Chase for help with my eyes, but he only laughed at me, and moved past us to set the pizza on the coffee table.

Grinning, Dorrie released me and moseyed away toward the couch. She sat and leaned back, still grinning.

I stepped toward the couch and sat beside her, then handed her the pardon to look over. "I expected you to be pleased, but not *this* pleased."

Still smiling, she looked over the paper, then turned her sparkling blue eyes to me. "I've been thinking a lot these past few weeks, especially with Chase working with Sam, and you working as a pack leader. I feel like I need a purpose, but I have no desire to return to my life as a *driver,* even if it were possible."

She paused as if in thought, so I took the opportunity to grab a piece of pizza from the box, then smiled down at Alexius as he came to beg at my feet. Pizza was his second favorite food, right after chicken strips. Chase sat beside me, grabbing his own slice and tearing off a small piece of crust for the dog.

"I really like alchemy," Dorrie continued, "and I think I'm pretty good at it. I gave Sam a few minor potions to sell to other demons, and he said they were excellent quality. I was thinking that maybe I could start selling them through Sam, but if the demon council isn't going to *unmake* me, maybe I can sell them myself."

I swallowed my bite of pizza, then turned to her with a smile. "I think that's a wonderful idea."

"Really!" she squealed, reaching out as if to grab me in a hug again, then thinking better of it. She placed the pardon on the table next to the pizza box, then continued, "I wouldn't know how to go about everything. I might need some sort of shop or office, but maybe if I can sell enough potions, I could afford to buy one."

I nodded as I swallowed another bite, appreciating her line of thinking. "I actually might have a proposition for you." I turned my eyes to Chase. "Though I'd wanted to talk to *you* about it first, before I started making any promises."

He raised an eyebrow at me, then set the slice of pizza he'd retrieved back into the box. "Should I be worried?"

I shook my head. "No, I was only waiting because I figured we could all use time to recover before jumping into anything."

He chuckled and put an arm around me. "Since when do we ever have time to recover?"

I laughed, placed my remaining pizza back into the box, then nestled against him. "I guess you're right. So you really want to hear about it right now?"

"Yes!" Dorrie answered for him.

I smiled at her, then turned my gaze back to Chase. "I've been thinking about things ever since we discussed me stepping down as pack leader. I've been trying to decide what I would like to do with my life moving forward. College is out, as are most mundane jobs since trouble seems to follow me around. I'm tired of endangering innocent people all of the time."

He frowned. "That's not your fault."

I shook my head with a soft smile. "I know, I'm not complaining, but it does factor into my plans. I've been thinking that I'd like to help people. So many members of the paranormal community are on their own. When there's trouble, they have no one to turn to."

Chase's eyes narrowed warily, but he nodded for me to go on.

"I was thinking that we could open a paranormal private investigation business," I blurted, unable to think of a better way to phrase it, "but not only would we solve mysteries, we could help people in other ways too." Afraid to hear Chase's opinion, I turned to Dorrie. "That's where you come in. Your alchemy shop could be part of it. A one stop shop for all of your alchemical and investigative needs."

Dorrie nodded excitedly. "So I'd get to work with you, Pop Tart?"

I nodded, then glanced back at Chase. "And maybe Chase," I continued hesitantly, "if he doesn't think I've entirely lost my mind."

My apprehension eased as Chase grinned. "I was *really* hoping I wouldn't have to work with my brother the rest of my life. I'd *much* rather work with the two of you."

I slumped against him in relief, but couldn't help adding, "You know, we might need his help from time to time. He *is*, after all, a record keeper of all things demonic."

Chase slipped his arm around my back, cupping

my shoulder, then pulled me toward him. He kissed my temple, then replied, "As long as it's not *all* the time."

I held up my hand in the salute for *scout's honor.* "Only when necessary," I assured.

"So when do we start!" Dorrie interrupted excitedly. "Tomorrow? Should we go and look for an office first? Or maybe we can make business cards!"

I cringed, and she suddenly deflated.

"We can do all of those things," I quickly promised, "I just have to take care of the werewolf business first. After everything that's happened, I have a feeling it might be difficult to convince Devin to take my place."

Chase gave my shoulders a squeeze. "Everyone wants to meet tomorrow regardless," he explained. "We can bring it up to them then."

I raised an eyebrow at him. "Since when did we have a meeting scheduled?"

He smiled, then reached forward to reclaim his slice of pizza. "No one wanted to bother you," he explained. "I was waiting for an opportune moment to tell you that everyone wanted to meet."

I leaned against him and sighed. I wasn't looking forward to the meeting, but it was necessary, especially since we weren't sure if Emma's abusive father had really been involved with *The Association.* He might still be lurking around Shelby, waiting for an opportune moment to steal Emma away.

"Okay," I breathed. "Tomorrow we'll discuss *everything.*"

Chase nodded, then retrieved the remote from the coffee table to flip on the TV. "Tomorrow it is, but *today* we relax and wait for our bruises to go away."

Speaking of bruises, I shifted and moved a throw pillow that had been pressing against my bruised side. I was well on my way to healing though, and so was Chase, because of our demon blood. Our scrapes had scabbed over, and our bruises had turned from black and blue, to pink, purple, and yellow. On the outside, we would heal up just fine.

Our insides were another matter. Could I ever really get over the horror of killing an entire compound of people? Would Chase's mind ever truly recover from being tortured?

I wasn't sure, but we would try. Our experiences would probably change who we were, but that wasn't always a bad thing. I may have run from change in the past, but I'd grown tired of running. I'd grown tired of always fighting. I was ready to just *be*.

I glanced first to Chase, then to Dorrie, both of their eyes intent on the TV as the movie started. We were all about to start our lives anew. It was scary, but also wonderful, because we'd get to do it together.

## Chapter 18

My mom was still out of town doing a biological survey, but she'd given me the okay over the phone to hold our meeting at her house. After two cups of morning coffee in the demon underground, Chase and I had left Dorrie and Alexius behind. Dorrie was going to start cleaning up the kitchen so we could have our morning coffee there instead of the den.

With cup number three in hand, I was nestled next to Chase on my mom's love seat. The living room was crammed full of people. On the couch, sat Lela, Allison, and Max. Lucy sat on the arm of the couch, a bandage visible beneath the collar of her shirt where the gunshot wound was. In dining room chairs moved to form a circle with the loveseat and couch were Abel, Devin, Jason, and even Sam. I hadn't expected Sam to attend, even though he *had* been part of everything. It was fine by me though, I'd rather just have to deliver my news once.

Emma and Siobhan weren't present. They were with the other wolves Devin had summoned to watch over them. Emma's father had been yet to show himself again, but we were still being cautious. If everything went according to plan, it would all become Devin's problem, should he choose to accept the role of pack leader. After everything that had happened, the chances were likely slim, but I had to try.

"I want to step down as pack leader," I announced suddenly, interrupting all of the quiet, murmuring conversations that were taking place.

Everyone turned to stare at me.

I bit my lip. "I, er . . . " I trailed off, realizing I really should have spoken to Devin privately. I met his eyes. "I was hoping that a replacement might volunteer. A replacement that likes it in Shelby, and is strong enough to run a pack."

He glared at me while everyone silently watched the exchange.

"This replacement would be very good at the job, especially since he likes bossing people around," I half joked.

The glare deepened.

I sighed. "But if he doesn't want to take over, I understand. I will remain in the role of pack leader until another suitable candidate is proposed."

He slumped back in his seat. "I'll do it," he muttered.

Abel raised an eyebrow at him. He looked just as bruised, battered, and tired as the rest of us, but still exuded his normal air of power and control. "Truly?" he asked, disbelief clear in his tone.

Devin nodded, then smirked at me. "It's only fair for me to take a turn. Xoe has done it long enough."

I grinned so wide my ears hurt.

Allison had obviously filled Max in, since he just smiled, not at all surprised, but Lela seemed worried. She'd gotten attached to me as leader. Being with our pack was the first time she'd ever really belonged, and I understood why a change might worry her.

I pulled my gaze away from her frightened expression, not wanting to draw attention to it and embarrass her. "I'll still be available in an advisory capacity," I announced to the room in general, though I spoke for Lela's benefit.

She visibly relaxed.

"In fact," I continued, "Chase, Dorrie, and I have decided to open up our own paranormal private investigation firm. We'd like to be available to help demons, and members of the paranormal community alike."

Jason raised an eyebrow at me. "So you're stepping down as pack leader just to become more involved in the paranormal community?"

I lifted a finger in the air as if to argue, but I couldn't. "Well yes, but now people will have to hire me and I'll get paid for it. And I can turn down any jobs that I don't like."

He nodded in satisfaction. "I wasn't arguing with your idea," he explained. "I think it's perfect. You can't ignore your role as a demon, but you can at least control it."

Abel cleared his throat and tossed his long black hair over his shoulder. If anyone else was going to stand in the way of me stepping down, it was him.

"I'm willing to let you out of your role with the coalition on one condition," he stated.

A snide comment came to mind, but since Abel was smiling, I sensed he wouldn't try to keep me in the position against my will. "Go on," I encouraged.

His smile widened. "I propose that you keep your pack on retainer for any jobs that might involve them. That way, the threat of demonkind remains behind the wolves, and the threat of the wolves remains behind *you*."

I grinned. "Deal."

With that settled, everyone started chattering about the new developments. Max pulled Chase into a conversation about soccer, and Lela, Allison and Lucy starting discussing the new pack dynamic, soon to be interrupted by an inappropriate innuendo from Sam.

I smiled, watching everyone as we all relaxed and sipped our coffee. That was, until Jason caught my eye, and nodded toward the front door.

I tried to keep my breathing even, afraid of what he might want to discuss alone. Would he blame me for making him kill all of those people in the hidden compound? Would he say this was all my fault for getting involved with the wolves to begin with?

I steeled myself, then stood. He followed suit, we made our way toward the front door. No one hindered us, unfortunately.

We walked outside onto the front porch and shut the door behind us, mugs of coffee in hand. My dark thoughts were joined by the sound of cheerful birds, glad that it was finally spring. Jason approached the swinging porch seat and sat, leaving room for me to sit beside him.

I sat gingerly, still a little sore.

I glanced at his calm expression, feeling increasingly anxious the longer we went without speaking. "I'm sorry for dragging you into everything," I blurted. "You shouldn't have had to kill all of those people, and I know it was all my fault."

He smiled softly at me, waiting for me to finish.

I looked down into my mug of coffee, wondering why he was so calm.

"I just wanted to say that I'm glad you've formed a goal for your future," he explained, "*and* I wanted to let you know that I'm going to be leaving Shelby."

I turned to him in surprise, sloshing coffee all over my hand. "Because of me?" I asked before thinking better of it. "I'm sorry for what I put you through, and I swear I'll never ask anything like that of you again."

He continued to smile serenely. "You can ask me for help any time you need. I'm going to Moab to work for Abel on slightly more . . . mellow tasks. I feel I could use a break from the action." He held up a hand to stop my next argument. "And it's *not* your fault. Just as you have chosen your life path, I need to choose mine, and I'm beginning to think I'm too old for the bounty hunting business."

"Kind of hard to be *too old* when you're going to live forever," I argued softly.

He chuckled. "You'll know what I mean once

you reach my age."

My eyes widened. I *hated* to be reminded that I might be immortal, just like my dad was . . . until he died.

"I've agreed to work for Abel for the next year," he explained, "then who knows?"

My heart felt suddenly achy. Even though I'd only seen Jason off and on lately, the idea of him going away hurt. It wasn't rational or even fair, but I couldn't argue with the pain in my chest.

He gently elbowed my arm to get my attention. "Cheer up. I'm sure you'll find all sorts of trouble to draw me back into."

I offered him a small smile. It was *good* that he was going, and I was also glad to know I'd have a friend if I really did turn out to be immortal. I'd need *someone* to hang out with when I was one hundred years old. Hopefully he and Chase would be over their tendency toward working behind my back by then.

I gazed out at the green grass of the front yard and sipped my cooling coffee. "Life is strange," I muttered.

He leaned his back against the swing comfortably, his eyes on a family of birds hunting through the grass for seed. "It sure is, but that's half the fun."

We sat like that for awhile, then eventually rejoined the others inside. Abel excused himself early, then the rest of us spent the day together, just an ordinary group of friends to anyone that might happen by to peek in a window.

If only they knew the truth.

# Epilogue

"It's crooked," I observed, standing back on the cobblestone street in the demon underground.

Chase looked down from his ladder, hammer in hand, and sighed. "It was straight the last time you said that, so if it's crooked now, it's your own fault."

"It's been crooked every time," Dorrie said from beside me, tapping her foot impatiently with her hands in the pockets of her paint-covered overalls.

I wore equally grungy overalls, with a bandana holding my hair away from my face.

Demons milled in the street around us, trying to take a peek at the new business without being overly obvious about it.

Chase turned back toward the sign with a sigh. "We're hiring someone else to put up the sign in the human world."

I crossed my arms and tried not to grin. "But that sign won't be as cool as this one, so it won't matter."

Chase started taking the sign down again as Dorrie and I watched. It read, *Minor Magics* in big, scrawling letters, then underneath, in a smaller font, *Your One-Stop Shop for all Your Paranormal Problems*. The sign for our office in the human world just read *M.M. Private Investigation*. Didn't want to give the humans too much to think about.

Chase refastened the sign after only moving it slightly. He glanced over his shoulder at us. "How about now?"

"Perfect!" Dorrie and I both said in unison.

With a sigh of relief, Chase finished securing the sign, then descended the ladder. He came to stand on my side opposite Dorrie, and placed an arm around my shoulders.

"Are you ready for yet another adventure?" he asked playfully.

I smirked and looked up at our new office. The start to our new life. I'd travelled to different realms, and been kidnapped multiple times. I'd dealt with ghosts, demons, and the loss of loved ones. I'd been to hell and back, and somehow had come out of it all alive. But was I ready for this?

I took Chase's hand in mine and smiled. "I was born ready."

# Note from the Author

Thank you for reading the final installment in the Xoe Meyers Series! Notice I said final installment? Well, don't kill me yet. I'm planning a spinoff series based around Minor Magics, the new detective agency, to be released in 2017. The new series will be a little more adult (since gasp, Xoe will finally be 18!), but will otherwise be a continuation of Xoe's story. In the mean time, I also have several other series available, including my Bitter Ashes Series, the first of which, can be read for free (digitally) on all platforms. I hope you'll consider checking it out! As always, please remember to leave a review, and for new release alerts, please sign up for my mailing list by visiting my site:

www.saracroethle.com